THE DISAPPEARING TV STAR

Sconeuer
Conserve
Onserver

5@

3 7 9 15 4 6 43 11

8 11 14 24 26 49 (45)

5 4

8 11 24 26

14 49

8 11 24 49

Raven Hill Mysteries

THE DISAPPEARING TV STAR

Raven Hill Mysteries 3

Emily Rodda
&
Mary Forrest

Hodder
Children's
Books

a division of Hodder Headline plc

First published in Australia in 1994 by
Ashton Scholastic Pty Limited

First published in Great Britain in 1995
by Hodder Children's Books

A Catalogue record for this book is available from the British
Library

ISBN 0 340 62994 0

Typeset by Avon Dataset Ltd, Bidford-on-Avon
Printed and bound in Great Britain by
Cox & Wyman Ltd, Reading, Berks.

Hodder Children's Books
a division of Hodder Headline plc
338 Euston Road
London NW1 3BH

Contents

1

Sucked in

I was on my way to meet the others when I saw the headline.

CASSANDRA CASS KIDNAP FEAR

Wow! Straightaway I grabbed a paper and paid over the money for it. Cassandra Cass—the hottest TV star around—kidnapped! How come I hadn't heard about this on the radio?

I read the story quickly and groaned. I'd been sucked in. It was a total fake.

Cassandra Cass hadn't been kidnapped at all, it turned out. She and her mother were just afraid that she *might* be kidnapped. By a mad fan, or someone after some huge ransom. They'd just come back from America where Cassandra had been working on a film. They'd heard about star kidnappings while they were away. Now, the paper said, they lived in fear.

'Oh, sure,' I muttered in disgust. 'She might be kidnapped. Or she might go bald overnight, or be visited by aliens from outer space, but I doubt it.'

I threw the paper in the bin, forgot all about Cassandra

Cass, and walked on down to the Glen to meet the Teen Power gang.

I wanted to see if they'd organised any work for us yet. The holidays had just started. For a few weeks, instead of trailing off to Raven Hill High to be bored to death every day, we could work and make some serious money.

I suppose I should say here that Teen Power Inc. is the name of our group's mini-employment agency. 'Six responsible, mature teenagers will tackle any job around your house, garden, shop or business'—that's what it says in our ad. We've done some weird jobs over the past few months, I can tell you.

Unfortunately, we've had some weird adventures too. Those I could have done without.

Still, the money's been very handy. And now I desperately needed more funds. I didn't have a thing to wear. We had to find a job quickly. An interesting job, preferably. Not too strenuous. And, for once, without trouble and mystery attached.

As I've said to Liz Free over and over since Teen Power started: 'It's money I need, Liz. Not trouble.' But she always groans and goes, 'Richelle, I don't understand you,' in that irritating way she's got. Sometimes I think Liz likes mess and danger as much as Sunny and the boys do. She certainly likes to make things complicated.

The Glen is this big block of land next to Raven Hill Park, with absolutely no houses on it, just a lot of prickly bushes and old trees. Gum trees, I suppose. Liz says it's how Raven Hill must've looked two hundred years ago, before our ancestors came and built all over it.

But Liz has a weird imagination. Believe me. I've known her ever since we were in kindergarten. She had a weird imagination then, too.

I stopped at the edge of the Glen. I wasn't going in unless I was sure that the others were there. The Glen's okay, quite peaceful and stuff, but it's spooky when you're on your own. Too quiet, and too many trees. And things rustle in the bushes. Besides, what's the point of getting your shoes messy for nothing?

So I called out: 'Anyone there?'

'No, Richelle,' a voice shouted back.

That was Tom Moysten, of course. Tom's always cracking jokes. Well, he thinks they're jokes. I never laugh.

'Very funny, Tom,' I yelled sarcastically, and started picking my way down the bush track.

The Glen's messy, but I have to admit it's a great meeting place. Most of the kids in Raven Hill stay away from it, because it's supposed to be haunted. And most of the adults in Raven Hill go to the park when they want to jog or walk their dogs or wheel their babies around in prams or something.

So we meet in the Glen, whenever we want to be private.

The gang was sitting around in the usual clearing. Tom Moysten. Nick Kontellis. Sunny Chan. Elmo Zimmer. (Liz should've been there as well, but for some reason she wasn't.)

As usual, Nick Kontellis had scored the most comfortable position, leaning against this big tree trunk. Nick has thick, dark hair and dark eyes and perfect skin and teeth. He's pretty cool. He's the total opposite to Tom, who's tall and skinny and clumsy like you wouldn't believe, and has braces on his teeth as well. Which probably explains why the two of them are always getting at each other.

I found a patch of reasonably clean grass and sat down. 'Any work yet?' I asked. 'We're wasting time.'

'I'm not,' Sunny Chan said. 'I'm training for that gymnastics competition. My coach reckons I've got a really good chance.'

For once Sunny looked almost excited. Normally, nothing much seems to show on her face. I don't know what goes on inside her, because she isn't exactly a close friend of mine.

If she *was* a close friend, I'd try and get her to do something about the way she looks.

Sunny could be really pretty. She's Chinese–Australian, so she has shiny, straight black hair, but she generally just ties it back in a ponytail. And she wears jeans and runners most of the time. Or tracksuits, if she's going to one of her never-ending classes. Gym, tae-kwon-do, yoga, you name something that gives you muscles and makes you sweat, and Sunny does it.

'Sunny,' I said patiently. 'That's not what I meant. I mean we're wasting time for Teen Power.'

'Actually, someone rang me about a job today,' Nick began. But Elmo Zimmer butted in.

'Hold on a minute, Nick,' he said. 'Let me just finish telling you about Dad's story.'

4

I'd forgotten about Elmo for a moment. He's easy to forget. Nick's good-looking already and Tom might be good-looking one day, when he stops growing and gets the braces off his teeth. But Elmo will always be little and chunky and red-haired and freckled and messy. I know that, because I've seen his father. Elmo's dad's called Elmo Zimmer, too (Zim for short) and he looks exactly the same as Elmo, only taller. Not much taller.

Zim runs the *Pen*, our local newspaper. It was started by Elmo's grandfather, whose name was—you've guessed it— Elmo Zimmer. So Elmo wants to run the *Pen* as well, when he gets old enough. He talks about it all the time. I usually tune out.

'It's about the new refuge in Raven Hill Street,' he was saying now. 'The place for homeless kids. Stephen Spiers interviewed some of them. You ought to hear the stories! Really bad.'

I yawned. I really was feeling tired, but straightaway Elmo stopped raving on and looked at me under his eyebrows.

I hate it when Elmo looks at me like that. As if I'm shallow, and selfish. I'm not selfish. I once sent half my allowance to this appeal that was advertised on TV, for these little kids who were starving in India or Africa or wherever. But you can't spend your whole life feeling sorry for people and getting angry about things that happen. At least I can't. Elmo can, though, and Liz is practically as bad.

'Go on,' I said with a sigh. 'Don't mind me.'

I wouldn't have been so nice about it if I'd known what

all this refuge stuff was going to lead to. Trouble. Again. For Teen Power Inc. and, more importantly, for me.

2

Big news

'The problem is,' Elmo began, 'some Raven Hill people don't want the refuge here. They're scared the kids'll start dealing in drugs or breaking into houses or something. But these kids aren't dangerous. Not the ones Stephen saw, anyway. They just need help. You should hear some of the stories, Richelle.'

'No, thanks,' I said with a shiver. 'Listen, Elmo, why are you telling us about this? Has the refuge got work for us, or something?'

Elmo frowned. 'Not exactly. But we can help. We can spread the word about it. About it being a good thing, and so on.'

I must have been staring at him, because he leaned forward and started trying to explain to me.

'Like, if your parents start talking about the refuge over dinner or whatever, you'll be able to tell them about it now, won't you?' he said. 'So they won't get the wrong idea.'

I grinned to myself. Elmo Zimmer has a pretty weird idea of family life. Maybe he and his dad talk about homeless kids

7

and politics and the problems of the world over dinner. But my family talks about the weather and TV shows and what we did during the day, like normal people.

'All right, we've got the picture. Can we get back to Teen Power now?' Nick asked, tapping his fingers impatiently.

I nodded hard. Nick and I mostly end up on the same side. I can trust him to bring Elmo and Liz back to earth whenever they get too carried away.

'The guy who runs The Palace rang me this morning,' Nick went on. 'He wants us to hand out leaflets about the holiday movie program.'

'Sounds okay,' Sunny said. 'It's easy work and . . .'

'Easy?' I groaned. 'Standing around in the street looking like dorks, forcing people to take pamphlets they don't want? And getting varicose veins and sunburn while we're at it? No way, Nick. Delivering the *Pen* on Thursday mornings is bad enough. Tell the Palace guy he can keep his job.'

I thought that would settle the whole thing. The others generally go along with my suggestions, which is reasonable, because I'm generally right.

But this time Nick didn't take any notice of me. 'Richelle, this is no time to be picky,' he said firmly. 'We haven't got anything else. And it's the holidays. The big money-making time. We need to take any job we can get.'

'That's right,' Elmo said. 'Besides, if we turn this Palace guy down, he won't come back. And he might tell other people we aren't worth trying. We can't afford that. What do you reckon, Tom?'

Tom never agrees with Nick if he can help it. I looked at him hopefully, but I was disappointed.

'Yeah, right,' he said. 'And we might get some free tickets as well as the cash.'

'Listen,' I argued, 'you haven't thought this through. Sure, we want work. But we want *interesting* work. We don't want the sort of work that anybody could do. We've all got special talents and we ought to use them. We should wait till something better comes along.'

'Like what?' Elmo said bluntly. 'No-one's offered to pay Tom for drawing cartoons, or Sunny for doing gymnastics, or you for giving them fashion advice.' He gave me that look again. 'Not lately, anyway. We get paid for walking dogs and minding kids and weeding gardens. Ordinary stuff like that.'

'Our ad does say "We'll Do Anything",' Tom put in. 'And, sad to say, Richelle, if we want money, and movie tickets, that's what we have to do. Life's tough in the big city.'

Sunny had become bored with the whole conversation. She found a low-hanging branch and held on to it, practising her leg-lifts. Tom noticed and started sketching her. They all make such a fuss of Sunny's gym stuff. I don't think they realise that dancers are just as fit as gymnasts.

I was just wondering whether I could get my leg quite as high as she could (naturally I didn't want to try in front of the others in case I couldn't), when she swung around.

'Here comes Liz,' she called.

I turned around and watched Liz pounding up the track towards us. A branch knocked her hat off, but she just grabbed it up and charged on. Typical.

I wished she'd left the hat where it was. She made it herself. It's blue crushed velvet, with a floppy brim. She loves it, but it looks like a shower cap gone wrong. Even though Liz has been around me for years and years, since we were both in pre-school, she has no clothes sense at all.

She struggled through the last bush and sank down beside us, gasping for breath. Liz has mid-length, mid-brown hair. Average height, average weight. My mother says she has an interesting face, but so what? I'd hate it if that was the best thing someone could say about me.

'Oh wow,' she burst out. 'You'll never guess what just happened.'

'Yes, I will,' Tom said. 'The Martians have landed. Look out, here they come!'

He pointed into the bushes. Branches heaved and Christo, Liz's dog, burst out, covered in leaves. He flung himself on Liz as though he hadn't seen her for a week.

Liz laughed and let Christo lick her face. I wrinkled my nose. I don't mind dogs in their place. But this particular dog really is just too—doggy. Huge and shaggy—and half the time wet.

'Come on, Liz,' I snapped. 'What's the big news?'

Liz paused for a moment, drawing out the suspense. 'I'm late because I got a phone call,' she began. 'From this advertising company. They've got a job for Teen Power. They're making a TV commercial for Markham & Markham.'

'The Chocko Bar people? Who also make Megatreat? And

Dreamy?' asked Tom. Trust him to be full of information on junk food. He was actually licking his lips at the thought of it.

'Yes,' said Liz. 'And now they've got this new thing. It's going to be called The Lot. It's got—hang on a minute.' She fished around in the pocket of her jeans and found a crumpled piece of paper. 'Chocolate, caramel, nuts,' she read out, 'nougat, marshmallow and coconut, all wrapped in a crunchy raspberry toffee coating.'

Tom looked hungry. Nick looked ill.

'That's gross,' he said. 'Well, if they want to test it out on us, you can count me out, Liz. I've got too much respect for my stomach. Tell them to get some lab rats. They're cheaper than us.'

'Can't afford to be picky, Nick!' yelled Tom. 'Like you said, we've got to take anything we can get.'

Nick shot him an unfriendly look. Sunny giggled.

'Oh, *no*!' exclaimed Liz. 'It's not that. They don't want us to test The Lot. It's already been tested. It's about to go on the market. They're making a TV ad for it, in Raven Hill Park. And they want . . .'

She paused again, and glanced at me, smiling. I looked down at my fingernails, pretending to be only half-listening. But I have to admit my heart had started to beat a bit faster. Could this job possibly be what I thought it was?

'*They want us to be in the ad!*' squealed Liz.

Yes! My heart pounded while the others chattered and exclaimed. I was going to be on TV. In an ad. This was the chance I'd been waiting for. The way in to being a model, and later, maybe, a film actress. I knew something like this would happen one day. I just knew it.

'Just as extras, of course,' Liz was babbling on. 'To back the main star. They especially want ordinary kids, see. They don't want professionals. So . . .'

'We'll be on TV?' Elmo broke in nervously. 'Look, Liz, I don't know if I can . . .'

'Don't worry, Elmo,' Liz said. 'It won't be hard. We don't have to talk, or do anything special. We just have to wear our ordinary clothes and play around in the background, while they film the main star.'

I took a deep breath. 'And who's the main star?' I asked, trying to sound calm.

'Wait till you hear!' Liz said, her eyes sparkling. 'You won't believe it! It's Cassandra Cass.'

3

Bad news
is good news

I looked around at the others. 'See?' I told them. 'You should've listened to me. I was right. We just needed to wait. This job is going to be heaps more fun than handing out leaflets.'

'I don't know,' mumbled Elmo, who was still looking nervous. 'I can't quite see myself as an actor.'

'Elmo, they don't *want* actors,' Liz reminded him. 'Jasmine, the woman from the advertising agency, was quite definite about that. They just want ordinary kids.'

Nick raised one eyebrow. 'Well then, you'll be fine, Elmo. Nobody looks more ordinary than you do.'

That's a typical Nick remark. I didn't know whether he was cracking a joke or insulting Elmo or simply stating a fact. Then he looked across at me and winked, so I decided that he was cracking a joke, after all.

Elmo didn't care, anyway. He was too busy worrying about the commercial. He rubbed his freckled face and tugged at his curly red hair until it stood up in spikes like corkscrews.

'Oh, all right,' he growled finally. 'I suppose it might be interesting to see how an ad's made.'

Trust Elmo to come up with a really boring reason for liking the job. I stared at him, wondering whether he was actually an alien in disguise.

'Is that all you can say?' I demanded. 'Aren't you the slightest *bit* interested in meeting Cassandra Cass?'

Elmo thought about it. 'Oh, sure,' he said finally. 'If we *do* get to meet her.'

'Of course we will,' burbled Liz. 'We'll be working with her. And she's bound to talk to us. She's not all that much older than us, is she?'

'She's nineteen,' I said. 'She's been acting since she was eight.'

'If you call it acting,' said Nick, looking down his nose.

Liz bristled up as if Cassandra Cass was her own personal invention. 'Well, *I* call it acting,' she said. 'She's a natural, my mother says. And she's so gorgeous-looking. Remember her in *Outback*?'

Nick shrugged. 'Yes. Unfortunately,' he sneered. 'And I saw her in *My Five Daughters* a couple of times, too. She was hopeless.'

'Anyway, whether you call it acting or not, she's done a lot of it, here and in America, and she's made a fortune,' Sunny put in flatly. 'They reckon she's a millionaire. A millionaire at nineteen.'

Nick stopped sneering. We were all silent for a moment, trying to imagine what it would be like. Unreal, I thought. If I was a millionaire, no-one would be able to boss me around. Even Mum and Dad. I could do whatever I liked and buy anything I wanted.

'This ought to be good,' Tom said, rubbing his hands together. 'She'll probably have bodyguards and everything, because of the kidnapping stuff.'

'Yes, isn't it awful?' Liz exclaimed. 'Poor thing. She's such a big star, and she's got all that money, but she's got no freedom at all. Imagine never being able to go anywhere on your own!'

'Do you think it's true, though?' I demanded. 'Would somebody *really* try to kidnap her?'

Nick sniffed. 'No. It's a lot of bunk. Cassandra Cass isn't that hot. Besides, this isn't Hollywood. I bet the whole story was just a lot of hype she made up.'

'Yes. Especially if she wants publicity at the moment,' Elmo said knowledgeably. 'It makes a better story if she's got a problem. Like Dad says, "Bad news is good news".'

'Don't be so cynical!' Liz protested. 'Cassandra Cass doesn't need fake stories to help her get publicity. She's news whatever she does. Everybody loves her. Old people and young people. You should have heard Jasmine raving about her on the phone. She says Cassandra Cass has universal appeal.'

'Well, she doesn't appeal to me,' Nick said flatly. 'She's an airhead. Whenever I saw her playing the kid in *Outback*, I used to want to throw up.'

'What about *My Five Daughters*, though?' Sunny asked. 'She was really cute in that.'

Nick made a gagging noise. 'Sure, if you like cute. The punk sister who hated everyone and had all the problems was much better. What was the name of the actress? Oh, yeah— Anna Wheat. At least Anna Wheat can act. Cassandra Cass just posed around, being sweet and wholesome and smiling at the camera. Dead boring.'

Tom looked as though he wanted to say something, but he didn't get the chance. Liz came rushing in to defend Cassandra Cass. Her cheeks were red and her eyes shone, the way they always do whenever she gets worked up about something.

'Why do people always say that good things are boring?' she demanded. 'It really annoys me. OK, Cassandra Cass is pretty and nice. What's wrong with that? Why would she be more interesting if she was nasty and horrible?'

'Relax,' Nick said with a grin. 'Don't get so mad about it. She's only a TV star.'

'Yes, and people only spend half their lives in front of the TV,' Liz raved on. 'And what do they watch? News about accidents and wars and disasters. Films about guns and bombs and car crashes. If someone builds a house, that's not news. If someone burns down a house, that *is* news. If you ask me, it's really sick.'

I wanted to point out that nobody had asked her. But

16

Elmo got in ahead of me.

'Come on, Liz,' he said soothingly. 'Think about it. Would you read a newspaper story that started, "The Free family had dinner together last night without having an argument, for the hundredth time in a row"? No, you wouldn't—and neither would anyone else. News has to be unusual and interesting. Like my dad always says . . .'

'Bad news is good news,' Tom and Sunny chanted together.

'Go on, make a joke out of it,' Liz yelled. 'But I'm right, just the same.'

She repeated everything she'd said, all over again. Nick sighed and started to tell her why she was wrong. Then the others joined in as well.

Finally Nick turned to me. 'What do you think, Richelle?'

'Me?' I answered. 'I think we ought to decide whether we're taking this job or not.'

'Of *course* we're taking it!' yelled Liz.

'Yes, I guess so,' Sunny said cautiously. 'As long as they're going to pay us properly. How much did they offer?'

Liz grinned and told us and we all gasped in amazement.

'All right,' Sunny said in a rush, '"I guess so" has just changed to "Yes, definitely".'

'Right,' Nick agreed. 'That's more money than we've ever earned from a single job.'

'Hey, it's peanuts, compared to what Cassandra Cass'll be earning,' Tom pointed out. 'She's never done an ad before,

17

you know. Markham & Markham must be paying her a fortune.'

'Then why are they using amateurs like us to back her?' Elmo asked, looking bothered again. 'I hope we won't wreck the whole thing.'

'Maybe they spent most of their budget on Cassandra Cass, so they need to do the rest of it on the cheap,' Sunny laughed. 'And if we wreck the whole thing—that's their problem, isn't it?'

They went on talking about Cassandra Cass and I drifted back into my own thoughts.

My heart had stopped thumping by now, but my whole body was still tingling with excitement. I didn't care about the money—although it'd be handy. No, what I cared about was something much more important.

This could be my big break.

I know I'm good-looking enough to be a model. I take care of my appearance. And I do dancing classes. Models and actresses need to look good and dress well and move beautifully. But they need something else as well.

Luck.

I've read all the interviews. Famous models and actresses always say they worked hard for their success. They talk about drive and dedication. And then they admit that they got their big break because they happened to be in the right place at the right time.

A famous photographer happened to come into a coffee shop where they were waitressing, for example. Or they had a small part in a TV show and some big producer happened to notice them. Or they were in a low-budget movie that turned into a runaway success.

In other words, they were lucky.

Still, I'm a fairly lucky sort of person, too. People are always saying so. And as far as I was concerned, this new job was proof of it. Cassandra Cass might be the star of the ad, but stars have been outshone by extras before. Lots of times.

I stared into the future and saw myself in a long, slinky dress, with reporters and photographers crowding around me, my name in lights, and some famous actor in a tuxedo guiding me through the crowd. People were waving and cheering. 'Richelle,' they were calling. 'Richelle! Richelle! Richelle . . . !'

4

Ready, set . . .

We heard about the ad on Saturday and the filming in Raven Hill Park was to start the next Tuesday. So I had only three days to make sure I looked my absolute best.

I began with my clothes. Luckily my second-newest jeans were just starting to look good. They'd faded well, and were tight enough without actually killing me when I bent over. And I'd decided to wear my new top, for certain. It matched my eyes perfectly. 'Forget-me-not blue'—that's how Dad describes the colour of my eyes. I wanted the director to remember me, so forget-me-not blue seemed like a good idea.

I did my nails and my eyebrows and tried all my skin creams. I washed my hair with my herbal lightening rinse six times between Saturday and Monday morning. By Monday afternoon it was looking really blonde.

At four Liz came around to show me what she was going to wear for the ad. An embroidered jacket from the local op shop. (Liz just doesn't *understand* about clothes.) And this *awful* flowery dress she loves. I couldn't talk her out of the jacket. But at least I persuaded her to wear a plain skirt and T-shirt with it, instead of the dress she'd planned on.

○

That night I went to bed really early, to get my beauty sleep, and at a quarter to seven next morning I was waiting on the front doorstep.

Dad drove me down to Raven Hill Park, on his way to work.

As we pulled in to the kerb, I could see a whole lot of people walking around near the playground equipment. There were four vans too, parked on the grass nearby, and lots of thick wires lying around. It all looked very, sort of, *official*. My mouth went dry.

Dad smiled at me. 'Off you go, princess,' he said, patting me on the shoulder. 'Knock 'em dead. You look beautiful. We're very proud of you, Mum and I.'

I nodded. Mum and Dad can be a real nuisance at times. Mum keeps raving on about family history and Dad keeps raving on about hardware. So irritating. Boring, too. Basically, though, they're pretty nice.

'Thanks, Dad,' I said and kissed him on the cheek. Then I got carefully out of the car, brushed the creases out of my jeans, fluffed my hair and walked casually over to the playground.

As I got closer I could see that it was a mess of cables and lights and equipment. There were cameras, and a big microphone thing, and black boxes with wires sticking out. There were some big white umbrellas planted here and there.

One of the vans was full of equipment. Another one seemed to be giving out coffee and food. A dozen cool-looking men and women were wandering around, chattering at each other and drinking mineral water out of bottles. They took no notice of me at all. It was all a bit scary, actually.

For once, I was glad to see Elmo Zimmer. He must've been glad to see me too, because he practically leapt out from under the tree where he'd been lurking, grabbed my arm and gasped, 'Richelle! You look great. How do I look?'

'Fine,' I said, without bothering to check. (Elmo always looks the same.) 'Where are the others?'

He looked helpless. 'I've just arrived,' he said. 'I've got no idea.'

'Yo, Richelle!' There was a Tom Moysten roar from the other side of the playground. I looked over and there he was, grinning and jumping and waving both arms above his head like some sort of madman. He was wearing this incredibly huge and bright green T-shirt he has. He looked *ridiculous*.

A few of the film crew stared at him and then at me. They murmured to each other, and smiled. I felt my face get hot. I wanted to be noticed, sure. But not this way. Tom really has no *idea* of how to behave. He's so embarrassing.

'Come on,' urged Elmo, almost jumping out of his skin with nerves. 'Liz and Sunny are there too.'

We hurried across the playground, jumping cables and dodging the crew. There were two more vans parked here.

22

Some little kids were gathered around one of them, talking to a plump blonde woman in a pink tracksuit, and an older girl sat on the steps of the van behind them. I ran my eye across the group and sighed to myself with relief. None of them were better-looking than me.

As Elmo and I joined the others, the tracksuit woman came bustling over. Close up you could see that she was older than she'd seemed at a distance. At least as old as my mother, I thought. She had waving, shoulder-length golden hair, and was wearing a lot of make-up.

'Hello,' she said, 'I'm Hazel Cass, Cassandra's mother. I always like to get to know everybody who's working with Cassie. Could you tell me your names, please?'

While Sunny was introducing herself, Hazel Cass looked at her more closely. 'I think I've seen you before, Sunny,' she said, smiling sweetly. 'In the shopping mall, perhaps?'

'Do you live in Raven Hill?' Sunny said in surprise, and Hazel laughed.

'Oh, no, no. Not usually,' she said. She gave the impression that the Cass family was rather above lowly Raven Hill.

I felt a finger tickle my ribs, and just managed to stop myself squeaking and making a fool of myself. I flicked my head around to see Nick, dressed all in black and looking very cool. He raised one eyebrow at me and I frowned at him.

'Cassie has three other jobs to do in the city over the next couple of weeks—including a very important casting session this Thursday,' Hazel Cass was explaining to Sunny. 'And we don't like hotels, not for weeks at a time.' She smiled around at us.

'So we're staying in a very dear old friend's house in Raven Hill while she's away overseas,' she went on, patting the back of her golden hair. 'That's one of the reasons why Raven Hill Park was chosen as the location for this shoot. So much more convenient for Cassie. I can't have her overtired.'

'Of course,' Nick said in my ear. 'Obviously everything has to be just *right* for dear little Cassie.'

'Shut up!' I hissed out of the corner of my mouth. 'She's her mother, you idiot!'

Nick raised an eyebrow again and straightaway turned on the charm. He can do it pretty well, when he wants to. Hazel Cass seemed very taken with him. She chatted to us for a while and then she went away to organise somebody else. We looked at each other, bubbling with excitement.

'This is great,' Elmo said eagerly. 'They're living here. Maybe I can get an interview with Cassandra Cass for the *Pen*. Teenage millionaire TV star in Raven Hill.'

'Yeah, that'd be a good follow-up to your story about kids in refuges,' Tom said with a grin. 'I can just see the headline. "Raven Hill—suburb of contrasts".'

He was joking, as usual, but Elmo took him seriously. 'You know, that's not such a bad idea, Tom,' he agreed. 'We could interview a homeless kid from the refuge. Then I could interview Cassandra Cass and we could compare the two lifestyles and backgrounds. That'd be great!'

'*If* you're allowed to interview Cassandra Cass,' I sniffed. 'I bet you aren't. She must be pretty heavily protected. Where is she, anyway? She should be here by now.'

Liz looked at me with a puzzled frown. 'She is. Didn't you see her?' She jerked her head. 'She's sitting over there.'

I turned around and stared hard at the girl sitting on the van steps. I'd barely noticed her before. She had a white, pointed little face and messy-looking fair hair. She wore a grey sweatshirt and faded jeans. She was small and pale and thin.

But she was Cassandra Cass, all right.

5

Lights, camera . . .

Cassandra Cass! What a major let-down. She was so *incredibly* ordinary-looking. Even worse than ordinary. Her skin obviously hadn't been exposed to the sun for years and years, so she was so pale that she looked quite sickly. (Still, I wished *I'd* been using sunblock for that long. I don't want to get wrinkles, like my mum.)

'That's Cassandra Cass?' I whispered to Liz. 'She isn't pretty at *all*.'

'I think she looks nice,' said loyal Liz. 'Those eyes! They're so blue—almost turquoise. And that gorgeous hair!'

I looked at the girl in disgust. 'She probably wears tinted contact lenses, you know, Liz,' I said. 'No-one has eyes that colour in real life.'

'Well, what about her hair?' Tom demanded. 'Don't tell me you think it's a wig, because I won't believe you.'

I checked Cassandra Cass again. She was smiling at one of the little kids now, and shaking her hair back off her shoulders. That mass of curly fair hair was her trademark, of course. But, come to think of it, fair hair generally gets darker as you get older. Mine did.

'I bet it's bleached,' I told Tom. 'Like her mother's. What a cheat. I'd never bleach my hair.'

(OK, I use that lightening rinse. It's not the same, though. It's herbal. Bleaching wrecks your hair. Cassandra Cass would probably be bald by the time she was twenty-five.)

'She still has a lovely smile,' Nick said, teasing me. 'That can't be a fake, can it, Richelle?'

I shrugged. 'Her teeth have probably been capped.'

'Oh, Richelle, stop putting her down,' Sunny said impatiently. 'What does it matter what she does? It's got nothing to do with us.'

I flicked back my hair and stretched, as if I wasn't paying any attention to her. It was all very well for Sunny. She didn't want to be a film star or a model. But how Cassandra Cass looked had a lot to do with me. After all, she was the star of this ad, and I was just an extra. It irritated me to see how fake her reputation for being some fabulous beauty was.

'And think about it, Richelle,' Nick murmured in my ear. 'No competition.'

I slapped him away and turned my back on him, but of course I'd been thinking the same thing. With Cassandra Cass looking like that it'd be easy for me to outshine her. Everyone would notice the contrast between us.

We hung around for a few minutes longer, and then Jasmine, the woman from the ad agency, introduced us to Luke, the director of the ad. He didn't spend much time with us, but he looked us all over, and I was convinced he looked longest at me.

Then Jasmine rounded us up and began sending us into a van, one by one, to have our make-up done. Cassandra had disappeared by now. She wasn't being made up with us. She had a van all to herself. She was being treated like a film star, even though all we were doing was making some little ad.

They had two make-up people—a guy called Warren, who did Liz, Tom, Nick, Sunny and Elmo, and a woman called Pat who came in at the end and did me.

I was a bit cross that I'd been left till last, but then it turned out that Pat had been in the other van all the rest of the time, working on Cassandra Cass. So she was obviously the senior make-up artist, and I'd been singled out for special treatment. I was pleased about that. I wondered if Luke had specially asked for me to be made up very well. Maybe he was planning to do some close-ups of me.

The van was crowded inside—an organised mess of wigs and clothes and hairdressing stuff and cases of make-up. It had one of those star mirrors with lights all around and a special chair that was a bit like a dentist's chair.

Pat was quite friendly, and talked a lot. But she was middle-aged and fairly plain-looking. Her teeth stuck out a bit at the front and her own hair and make-up weren't so wonderful. I hoped she knew what she was doing. I leaned back in the chair and tried to relax and pay attention to the way she used the colours. I thought I might pick up some good tips.

When she'd finished I wasn't quite sure if I liked the effect at first. She'd used much redder lipstick on me than I'd ever use. And she'd messed my hair around quite a bit, and sprayed it so it felt hard to touch. But my eyes looked good. And I could see in the mirror that I looked more glamorous than I had before.

I floated down the steps of the van, feeling good. The gang were standing together beside the playground. I waved at them, expecting them to be impressed, but they weren't even looking at me. They were too busy staring at Cassandra Cass.

She was standing on the grass next to the playground, smiling a dazzling smile for the camera.

Her golden hair was puffed out and floating around her shoulders in a mass of little curls. She was wearing full make-up. And she'd changed into a short blue dress. Forget-me-not blue, just like my top, except that her dress, although it looked casual, was far more expensive and well-cut than anything I'd ever owned. She uses fake tan, I thought, looking at her long, brown legs and golden shoulders. But the idea didn't make me feel any better.

Because Cassandra Cass didn't look like the pale girl on the van steps any more.

She looked stunning.

'Look, Richelle,' Liz mouthed.

She pointed to a TV screen on a stand with wheels. I peered over her shoulder. There on the screen was Cassandra Cass in her blue dress.

29

'That's the monitor,' Elmo explained. 'It shows what the camera's filming.'

I gazed at the picture in amazement, then glanced up from the screen to Cassandra Cass in the flesh, and back again. The girl facing the camera on the grass in front of me looked really beautiful. But on the TV monitor, she looked fantastic. Her eyes seemed enormous. Her skin was creamy, with a faint blush of pink. Her smile was radiant as she lifted her chin and raised a golden arm to touch the back of her hair.

And there was something else, something I couldn't describe.

'The camera loves her,' Elmo said suddenly. 'She looks a hundred times better on film. And watch the way she moves. She's so relaxed. You'd think she was going for a walk on her own.'

It was true. Cassandra Cass was surrounded by lights and cameras and white umbrellas, with a director talking to her non-stop, and yet she seemed to smile and pose in a totally natural way.

'What a professional,' Nick said admiringly.

I turned away from the monitor to glare at him. Four days ago he'd claimed to be bored by the whole idea of meeting Cassandra Cass. An airhead, he'd said. Nowhere near as good as Anna Wheat. Now, in the space of half an hour, he seemed to have forgotten all that.

OK, he wasn't drooling and goggling at Cassie the way Tom was. All the same, his cool, brooding expression didn't fool me. That's the look he always puts on when he wants to impress someone.

Right at that minute, he was obviously longing to impress Cassandra Cass.

Just then the director called us over. 'All right, kids,' he told us, 'I'd like you to fool around in the playground for a bit, while I decide what I want you to do. Don't look at the cameras at all. Just pretend we're not even here.'

I gulped. All of a sudden my chest was tight with nervousness. My knees started shaking. And I had an awful feeling that I was going to be sick.

6

Action!

Quickly I headed for the swings. I'll be safe there, I thought. And swinging will show off my long legs. Liz obviously had the same idea. Not about the long legs, of course, because her legs aren't particularly long, but about having something simple to do. She'd already bagged one swing when I got there.

The little kids were fine. They rushed over to the roundabout and climbed onto it, giggling wildly. Elmo went stiff and awkward straightaway, which wasn't a big surprise. But Nick looked very self-conscious as well, and I wouldn't have expected that. Mr Cool wasn't so cool once he was in front of the cameras.

I was checking out how Liz was looking on the other swing, when Luke called, 'Hey, you! The girl in the blue top. Ah, Richelle!'

Oh wow, I thought, letting the swing slow down. It's happened already. I've been discovered. He's going to tell me I've got star quality.

But he didn't say that at all. Instead, he told me that my

top was the same colour as Cassie's dress, so it had to go. He wanted me to change into a red shirt that Pat brought from the wardrobe van.

Instantly, I freaked. I knew I shouldn't throw a tantrum but I couldn't stop myself. Red isn't my colour. I *couldn't* wear a red shirt, I told him. No way.

Luckily, the guy behind the camera saved me. He told Luke that my top would actually pick up and highlight the colour of Cassie's dress. Luke checked the monitor again, thought for a minute, and finally agreed. He even gave me something special to do. When Cassandra Cass bit into the candy bar, Liz and I were supposed to jump down from the swings and run across to the slide.

Liz looked pretty uncomfortable running in her stupid jacket, but I didn't do too badly. I think I did it about as gracefully as possible. Still, by the time I reached the slide, my knees were trembling so much I could hardly stand up.

We had to keep on doing the same things over and over. It took hours! I got terribly tired. And Luke was quite bossy and impatient sometimes. It wasn't nearly as much fun as I'd expected it to be. And the fact that most of the others were really hopeless was a drag, too.

Tom was playing the fool, of course. It's impossible for him to take anything seriously. So he just did all these embarrassing things, like hanging upside down so his T-shirt fell all over his face, and juggling with the candy bars, half of which fell on the ground. I kept as far away from him as possible.

He was really gross. He even ate half a dozen The Lots. No-one could understand it. We'd all had a taste when Jasmine brought the bars out and they were *disgusting*. Even a dog that ran off with one of them spat it out.

The trendy advertising people, I noticed, kept telling the client, Mr Vincento from Markham & Markham, how delicious The Lot was—but they didn't eat any of the bars. They stuck to their mineral water and healthy stuff from the catering van.

Tom was the worst, but the others weren't much better. Except for one.

Elmo wandered around looking silly, and trying to look casual, and looking at the monitor, which we'd been told over and over again not to do.

Pat had to keep putting powder on Liz's face, because she went all red with nerves and the heat of her jacket, and stayed that way.

Nick was much too interested in being cool to play around like Luke wanted, so he was a bit of a washout.

But Sunny was a surprising success, I must say. She played on the bars, doing one of her gym routines. Luke loved her, because she followed his orders as easily as Cassandra Cass did. Sunny has always had iron nerves. She's not sensitive, like me. That's probably why I got more nervous than she did.

Anyway, I didn't really care about all that, because it was

completely obvious after the first ten minutes that Luke wasn't really concentrating on us at all. And neither was Mr Vincento, or anyone else. They were spending all their time and energy on Cassandra Cass. We were just faces in the background to them. Ordinary kids.

Cassandra Cass was the one with 'the lot', according to the ad. She was the symbol of that disgusting candy bar. Well, if that was what she got for being famous and bleaching her hair, she could have it, in my opinion.

Over the day we got to see quite a bit of Cassie (she asked us to call her that). We often had to stand around for ages, waiting for planes to go past overhead or clouds to move away from the sun, and at these times everybody automatically gathered around the star.

Close up, she looked really fragile and delicate and angelic, just like all the girls she played on TV. Tom couldn't keep his eyes off her. And neither could Nick.

I didn't like her at all.

The truth was, Cassie's little girl image was a big act. Tom and Liz and Nick thought she was wonderful. Sunny and Elmo still thought she was a bit of an airhead. But I thought she was tough and competitive and really sure of herself. She loved having an audience around her. And all her stories were about how terrific she was, even though she made out that she was being modest.

For example, during the lunch break, she told us about the audition she was doing on Thursday. She wanted the part so much, she said. It was the main role in a new drama series.

'I want to be taken seriously as an actress,' she said, frowning prettily. 'I know I'd be perfect for the part. I know I can do it. But they're looking at other actresses as well. Like Anna Wheat.'

She frowned even harder. Nick gave her one of his cool, brooding stares.

'Anna Wheat?' he repeated. 'But she's nowhere near as good as you.'

I sighed heavily, but he didn't flicker.

'Thanks, Nick,' Cassie smiled. 'You're really sweet. But unfortunately a lot of people don't agree with you. Just because Anna's a brunette and takes herself so seriously and never smiles, everyone thinks she's interesting and deep and a great actress. They've been raving about her ever since she did that part as a teenage runaway in *On the Streets*.' She sighed.

'I've always been typecast as a sweet, innocent young thing . . . but I've got more to give than that,' she said.

'You've spent most of your life acting, haven't you?' asked Elmo, obviously thinking about his interview for the *Pen*.

Cassie nodded. 'I didn't really have a childhood,' she said, looking down at the ground and fluttering her eyelashes. 'I hardly have any friends my own age.'

She clasped her hands and looked up appealingly, her big blue eyes serious. 'I envy all of you, you know,' she burst out. 'You're so free!'

The others were riveted. She had them right where she wanted them.

She bit her lip, as though she was getting her emotions under control. 'Anyway, tell me more about this Teen Power thing of yours,' she said, brightly and bravely. 'What's your next job, after this?'

The others rushed to tell her about how we planned to hand out leaflets for the local cinema, except we hadn't contacted the cinema owner yet. I felt seriously embarrassed. Cassie was a major star. She couldn't possibly be interested in all the trivial details of our lives. She was just practising on us. Stringing us along.

Compared to Cassie, the gang seemed really young and naive. Even Nick. She had them all in the palm of her hand.

She listened to Elmo raving about the *Pen* refuge story with her head on one side, looking concerned. She turned him down when he asked to interview her, but she did it so sweetly that he practically thanked her. Then she went into raptures about Liz's terrible op shop jacket. Liz was totally taken in, but I could tell that Cassie was just pretending.

After a while Hazel Cass came hurrying over. 'Cassie, they're going to start shooting again in a minute,' she said. 'Pat should freshen up your make-up. Do you need to go to the loo? Don't forget to spit out that awful Lot stuff between takes, will you?'

She turned to us, smiling. 'Chocolate isn't good for our skin, you know, and we have to watch our weight,' she whispered.

Cassie pulled a face, but she stood up obediently and went off to the make-up van. Hazel watched her go, smiling fondly.

'Cassie and I are each other's best friends,' she told us. 'I wanted to be an actress myself, forever ago, but I never made it. It's wonderful to see Cassie fulfilling both our dreams.'

When Hazel Cass bustled off to find Luke, Liz looked around at us, her cheeks red and her eyes shining.

'Poor Cassie,' she said. 'I feel so sorry for her. Her mother's running her life.'

Liz is always feeling sorry for somebody or something. Mind you, she's never been sorry for a teenage millionaire before. Even Sunny, who's her best friend, thought she was going a bit far with this one.

'Cassie's got a choice,' she shrugged. 'She's old enough to decide what she wants to do with her life. She doesn't have to be bossed around by her mum if she doesn't like it.'

Nick laughed. 'Listen, Cassie knows exactly what she's doing. She gets Hazel to do all her dirty work for her, while she smiles sweetly at everyone. It's pretty smart, really.'

I listened to them talking and arguing, and rolled my eyes. What does it matter what you think, I said under my breath. Cassie couldn't care less.

Still, when we went back to work, I realised I was watching Cassie more carefully than before. I noticed how she sucked up to Luke and the producer and Mr Vincento. I saw her go through the same moves, over and over again, without complaining. I began to imitate the way she glided from the hip and the way she flicked back her long hair.

Cassie was teaching me something, after all. You needed more than luck, to be a top star. You needed to have a tough streak and you needed to be keen on hard work.

I wasn't sure if I could ever be as tough as Cassie.

7

Trouble—again!

The shoot took an amazingly long time. A day's filming, for a minute of TV. Pat told us there were always a lot of hassles with outside shoots. Dogs, council clean-up vans roaring past, toddlers, falling leaves, rain. And all of the people who came along to watch, of course, including two guys in a van who hung around for most of the day.

They both had slicked-back hair and moustaches and they wore sunglasses and flashy *Miami Vice* style suits, with loads of gold jewellery. One of them had a camera and wandered around taking pictures from time to time.

'Journalists,' sighed Cassie during one of the breaks. 'They're probably here because of that silly kidnap story. I wish they'd leave me alone.'

I got the impression that Cassie didn't take the kidnapping threat very seriously. Maybe it was a beat-up, organised by her mother. Maybe Hazel had even told the press that Cassie would be in Raven Hill Park today.

But at one point, when the reporters came closer than

usual, Hazel raced over to warn Cassie to stay away from them. 'I don't mind them getting a few pictures,' she said. 'You mustn't give them an interview, though. I've promised the next story to *Top TV*.'

Cassie looked fed up. 'More kidnap stuff, I suppose,' she said to us with a groan after her mother had gone.

We spent two-thirds of the day shooting the ad. Then the sky clouded over and we had to stop. Cassie had finished her bit, but the rest of us would have to turn up again next day. Nick was pleased. All day he'd been wishing that he'd brought his video camera along to get some pictures of all of us with the crew. Now he'd have his chance.

'I'm exhausted,' Tom moaned. 'Which is weird, because we've spent most of the day standing around doing nothing.'

'Yeah, I can't understand how come Cassie still looks so fresh,' Liz said, watching her as she chatted with her mother. 'She's really amazing, isn't she?'

'She's a professional,' Nick reminded her. 'A real professional.'

At that point Hazel left Cassie and wandered casually over to Mr Vincento, the man from Markham & Markham. She was probably planning to talk him into using her daughter for some more candy bar ads, I thought.

'She never stops,' Cassie said wearily, coming over to us.

Looking at her close up, I could tell she was tireder than

she looked. I suppose it's all part of the job—smiling at people when you just want to go and have a sleep.

'Listen, will you wait for me for five minutes?' she said. 'I have to go and take my make-up off and get changed now because Pat wants to pack away. But I'd love to chat to you a bit more.'

We waited for her, of course. But when she came back in her sweatshirt and jeans, and with a bag over her arm, Hazel pounced on her straightaway.

'I've been having a lovely chat to Tony Vincento, Cassie darling,' she gushed. 'He's asked us to come to the Black Cat for a coffee, so we can finish our discussion in comfort. So hurry up, now. He's waiting.'

Cassie shook her head violently, until her fair hair fluffed out in a halo. 'Please, Hazel,' she begged. 'Not today. I'm so tired. I just want to go home.'

Hazel hesitated, looking torn. 'Now, you can't just change your mind like that, Cassie,' she murmured, glancing at us in case we were too interested. 'I've got Tony all warmed up and keen. I can't possibly let him go now. You know how important he could be to us.'

'Well, you have coffee with him, then,' snapped Cassie. 'I told you. I want to go home!'

Hazel frowned. 'You know I can't let you walk home on your own, Cassie,' she said. 'It's far too dangerous.'

She put her arm around her daughter's shoulders and turned her away from us. They started to argue together in whispers. Cassie flounced and stuck out her bottom lip. Hazel talked at her and pleaded with her and ticked her off, keeping an eye on Mr Vincento all the time.

After a couple of minutes of this, Liz couldn't help herself. She stepped forward. 'Excuse me, Hazel,' she said in her politest voice. 'Would it help if we walked Cassie home, while you go with Mr Vincento?'

Cassie smiled gratefully. Her mother hesitated. She was obviously embarrassed at being caught out bullying her daughter.

'Oh, well, I *suppose* that'll be all right,' she said grumpily at last. 'Go straight to the house, though, Cassie. And don't forget to lock the door behind you.'

The minute she turned away, Cassie grabbed Liz's arm. 'Thank you,' she gasped. 'But it's ridiculous, isn't it? Imagine a group of schoolkids having to walk me home!'

She turned away. 'I'm so *sick* of being treated like a child,' she raged. 'I'm nineteen years old, for heaven's sake! Mum's just being so *stupid* about this kidnapping thing.'

❂

I was looking forward to walking through Raven Hill with Cassandra Cass. With a bit of luck, we might run into some of our friends from school. Or my sister Tiffany—that would be even better. She'd practically die of jealousy if she saw me chatting away with a famous TV star.

But, as it turned out, I didn't see anybody I knew. I didn't even get to hear any hot gossip about Hollywood stars. Cassie just raved on about her mother the entire time. We had to listen in total silence while she told us how bossy Hazel was, and how she was a slavedriver and over-protective, and was running Cassie's life as well as her career.

After we'd watched Cassie go into the house and lock the door, we all went straight home. Nick mumbled something about the guy at the Palace, but we were all exhausted and decided to follow up on that job the next day, if the shoot ended in time.

I stumbled through the front door and heard Mum messing around in the living room.

'Is that you, Richelle?' she called. 'Oh, you're nice and early. I wasn't sure what time you'd be finishing. How did it go?'

I thought about how Hazel fussed over Cassie non-stop. And I ran into the living room and gave Mum a big hug.

She looked surprised. 'What's that for?' she asked. 'Not that I'm complaining, of course.'

'Nothing special,' I said. 'Just—thanks.'

❂

Mum had cooked a great meal to celebrate me being in the ad, but I could hardly stay awake for it. I went to bed straight after dinner and I was almost asleep when Tiff came and hammered on the door.

'Go away,' I said drowsily, but she marched in and pulled the covers off me.

'Blame Liz Free,' she said with a smirk. 'She told me to

wake you up if I had to. She reckons it's urgent.'

I staggered to the phone and picked it up. 'Liz, I was *asleep*! What's the matter *now*?' I snapped.

Liz gulped noisily. 'Oh, Richelle,' she wailed. 'It's terrible! Jasmine rang me. Apparently, when Hazel Cass got home late this afternoon, Cassie's door was closed, and she thought she was asleep. But a while ago she checked. And Cassie wasn't in her room at all! She's nowhere in the house. She's vanished!

8

Fuss
and bother

I groaned. Why did everybody always make such a fuss about Cassandra Cass? As if Hazel Cass wasn't bad enough, now Liz was joining in.

'Calm down,' I yawned. 'So Cassie's gone out for a while. What's that got to do with us?'

'A lot,' Liz shot back. 'Hazel thinks she's been kidnapped. And we were the last people to see her, Richelle! Jasmine rang because Hazel wanted to know whether we watched her go into the house.'

'Well, we did. She went inside and locked the door. End of story.'

I was just being practical, but Liz was all stirred up. 'How can you be so cold-hearted, Richelle?' she yelled into the phone. 'Don't you understand? Cassie's gone. She probably *has* been kidnapped, just like Hazel says. You saw her today—you know how sweet and helpless she is. Don't you feel the slightest bit worried about her?'

Maybe, I thought. But then again, maybe I felt more sorry for the kidnappers. Knowing Cassie, she'd probably turn them into leading members of the Cassandra Cass Fan Club within a few hours. If she'd been kidnapped at all.

'Listen, Liz,' I said reasonably, 'if you ask me, Cassie just decided to get away from her mother for a while. Remember on the way home, how she kept raving on about how Hazel drove her crazy? She probably thinks she'll get back at her by disappearing—and maybe get a bit more publicity at the same time.'

'That's what Sunny and Nick said too,' Liz told me reluctantly.

'Well then, what did you ring me for?' I exploded. 'Stop panicking. Cassie'll turn up. In fact, she's probably back home arguing with Hazel and having whatever millionaires have for dinner right now, while you're carrying on and keeping me awake!'

Liz wasn't convinced. She rambled on for a while, working herself into a state again, but finally I managed to get her to stop and say goodbye.

I crawled back to bed and fell asleep within thirty seconds.

✿

Next day we were back at the park by seven. Nick was already walking around with his video camera fixed to his eye. Elmo was on a high, because one of the big city papers had picked up the *Pen*'s story about the Raven Hill kids' refuge. He had the paper with him and he insisted on showing it to everyone.

I read the headline, 'Home for the Homeless', in big capital letters, and then ran my eye over the story.

'But it doesn't say anything about the *Pen*,' I said.

'Of course it doesn't,' Elmo answered, staring at me. 'That's not the point, Richelle.'

I shrugged. 'What *is* the point, then?' I whispered to Nick. He'd quickly lost interest in the refuge story and was standing beside me, messing around with his video camera. I couldn't for the life of me see why Elmo would be pleased. It wasn't as if his father had his name in the paper, or anything.

'He likes the idea that *The Morning Mail* thinks a *Pen* story is worth stealing,' Nick muttered out of the corner of his mouth. 'He thinks it's flattering.'

Oh. How odd, I thought.

Just then, Liz came hurrying over to us. Elmo pounced on her and thrust *The Morning Mail* into her hands. She looked at it, and congratulated him and everything, but I could see that her heart wasn't in it. She had other things on her mind.

'Any news about Cassie?' she demanded, as soon as she could decently get out of Elmo's clutches.

'No-one here's said anything,' said Tom.

'She must have turned up,' said Elmo, rather put out because Liz hadn't fussed enough about his refuge story hitting the big time. 'There's nothing in the paper.'

'That doesn't mean anything!' Liz exclaimed. 'They could be keeping it quiet. Come on, let's go and ask Pat. If anyone knows, she will. She always seems to know everything.'

Pat was busy in the make-up van, sorting through a tangled pile of wigs, shirts and scarves. I noticed the red shirt I'd refused to wear on the top of the pile. I shuddered. That had been a lucky escape.

'This van was perfectly tidy yesterday and now look at it,' Pat complained. 'Warren hasn't been packing away as he goes. No, Liz, I don't think Cassie has turned up yet. But I wouldn't worry about it too much. Luke says for sure she just stormed off somewhere to give her mother a scare. They had that big argument yesterday, remember? Everybody saw them.'

'Told you,' I muttered to Liz. 'Stop carrying on about it, Liz. It's embarrassing.'

But Liz didn't take any notice of me. 'It just doesn't seem like the way Cassie would behave,' she insisted. 'What does Hazel think about it?'

Pat laughed. 'Oh, you know Hazel. She's hysterical. She called the police straightaway last night, but they didn't do anything, of course.'

'Why not?' Liz demanded.

Pat shook her head and went back to her tidying up.

'For one thing, Liz,' she said patiently, 'Cassie's clothes and bag were in the bedroom and a wet towel was lying on the floor of the bathroom. So she'd obviously showered and changed before she went out again. And there was no sign that anything unusual had happened in the house. No sign of a struggle. No reason to think she didn't go out quite of her own free will.'

'Nothing suspicious at *all?*' Elmo asked in his junior reporter voice.

'Well, there was one strange thing,' Pat admitted. 'Cassie's wallet had been left on the dressing-table in her room. But she could've easily tucked some money into her pocket before she went out. She'd taken her keys, anyway— Hazel noticed that they were missing.'

'OK, well, maybe she did go off to get a bit of time to herself,' Liz said, relaxing slightly.

'Yes. And, personally, I think that's great,' Pat announced. 'She's nineteen years old. She should be free to come and go as she pleases. It's time she learnt to stand up to that mother of hers. Now. Who's first for make-up?'

❖

Without Cassie around, it was a lot easier to relax, although it was a lot less interesting too, in a way. But at least today everyone was just concentrating on us. Once they got to know us better, the crew started to joke and kid around and soon we all started to have fun instead of feeling nervous all the time. Everyone except Elmo, that is. He even froze up in front of Nick's video camera.

I felt really on top of things, especially after one of the camera guys (his name was Dallas) said I photographed well. My only real problem was Tom, who was still being an absolute dork, but I managed to keep away from him quite easily, without it seeming too obvious.

It was still early, but already a small crowd had gathered to watch the filming. Word about the shoot must have spread since yesterday. Luke said not to look at the people, but of course I couldn't help glancing at them a few times. They were pointing to us and whispering to each other. It really gave me a taste of what it must be like to be a real star.

We had a short break, and Nick started filming the crowd, and the crew. The crowd got all excited about this, and the crew played up to them.

Luke started to shout orders at Nick, as though he was a real camera operator. Everyone was laughing. Then suddenly Hazel Cass strode into the middle of the group and stood furiously looking around.

'Well,' she said sarcastically. 'I'm *so* glad to see you're all enjoying yourselves!'

9

Suspicion

The laughter stopped as if a tap had been turned off.

Hazel was wearing a black tracksuit this time, which made her look very grim and tragic. She wasn't wearing any make-up, and her eyes were red as though she hadn't had any sleep, or had been crying.

'I'm glad you're enjoying yourselves,' she said again. 'I'm glad you aren't letting my poor daughter's abduction upset you at all.'

Her voice choked up and she stopped, biting at her lips.

'Hazel, I'm sure Cassie's all right,' Luke said quickly. 'She'll turn up soon. Remember what the police said. Most teenage runaways come back within the first twenty-four hours.'

Hazel recovered instantly. 'Cassie isn't a runaway,' she spat. 'She's been kidnapped. How many times do I have to say that? Why won't anyone believe me?'

Behind Hazel's back, Pat rolled her eyes at us. 'I think I know what's going on here,' she whispered. 'Mother Cass is on the publicity trail again. She's acting her socks off—and she always was a lousy actor.'

Meanwhile Luke was trying to calm Hazel down. 'Hazel, I know you're worried,' he was saying. 'But it really doesn't seem likely that Cassie's been kidnapped. The police said that there was no evidence of that at all.'

'Evidence?' Hazel Cass cried dramatically. 'Well if it's evidence you want, here it is!'

She flung out her arm and slowly opened her hand. On her palm lay a small white plastic case, with two round lids. We all stared at it, puzzled.

'That's a contact lens case,' Pat said finally. 'But why . . .?'

'Exactly!' Hazel interrupted furiously. 'These are Cassie's contact lenses. She sometimes takes them out when she's at home, but she'd never go out without them. Never! Not willingly, at any rate.' Her lips began to tremble again.

'Oh, no!' gasped Liz. But Hazel turned on her.

'Don't pretend to be upset, young lady,' she snapped. 'Cassie wouldn't be in trouble now if you hadn't interfered and persuaded me to let her go home with you yesterday. You and your friends.' She blinked back angry tears.

'You all thought you were so smart!' she accused, glaring around at us. 'You thought you were rescuing her from her interfering, over-protective mother, didn't you? I suppose you laughed about it between yourselves. Well, now you see!'

Luke started murmuring to her, but she brushed him aside and raged on while we shrank away from her.

'You—you—people like you don't know a *thing* about people like Cassie,' she shouted. 'You've got no *idea* what an innocent she is.' She pointed a shaking finger at Liz.

'I trusted you to look after her and now she's in terrible danger. I feel it. I know! And it's all your fault!'

Instantly the Teen Power gang moved closer together. Sunny put her arm around Liz's shoulders and Elmo scowled ferociously at Hazel Cass.

'You'd better check your facts, before you start saying things like that, Mrs Cass,' Nick said coolly.

I looked at him admiringly. Somehow Nick always knows the right thing to say. The angry spark in Hazel Cass's eyes flickered and went out. She licked her lips, and forced herself to smile at us.

'I'm sorry, Liz,' she said more calmly. 'I didn't mean to accuse you of anything. I know you liked Cassie—and Cassie liked you too. But you don't understand her the way I do. Cassie may be nineteen but inside she's just a baby. She's lived such a protected life that she has no idea of how dangerous the world can be.'

She straightened her shoulders. 'If the police don't take action soon, I'll take the story to the newspapers,' she said. 'The press love Cassie. They'll do anything to help.'

She swung around and went marching away.

'Phew!' Tom exclaimed. 'I'm glad she's decided that the police are the bad guys, not us. That woman scares me. I don't blame Cassie for running away.'

'But did she run away?' Elmo asked, frowning. 'I thought she did . . . until I saw those contact lenses.'

'Yes, the contact lenses are a worry,' Sunny agreed.

'Cassie wouldn't get far on her own if she was blind as a bat.'

We stared at each other miserably. Liz looked as though she was about to burst into tears and I didn't feel all that great myself. OK, I didn't like Cassandra Cass very much. Still, I wouldn't want my worst enemy to be snatched by kidnappers.

'What's the matter?' Pat asked, coming up behind us. 'Look, don't take Hazel too seriously. She's just blowing off steam. She doesn't mean half the things she says.'

Liz bit her lip. 'Thanks,' she said in a shaky voice. 'But you saw those contact lenses. Hazel wasn't making them up.'

'Not entirely,' Pat said with a smile. 'The contact lenses are real enough—but Cassie has perfect eyesight. She doesn't need contact lenses for seeing with. Those lenses are just tinted glass, to highlight the colour of her eyes. Hazel makes her wear them whenever she's in public, but Cassie told me they make her eyes sore. She could easily have decided to leave them behind, especially if she was annoyed with Hazel.'

Elmo gave a huge sigh of relief and the others looked a bit happier as well. I turned my head aside to hide a secret grin. I always knew those turquoise-blue eyes of Cassie's were too good to be true.

'So there you are, kids,' Pat said. 'You don't need to blame yourselves any more. Cassie will turn up any time now. After all, she's got that casting session tomorrow afternoon. She certainly won't let Anna Wheat have it all on her own.'

Liz waited until Pat had gone and then she shook her head.

'I think Hazel's right, all the same,' she whispered. 'Cassie is pretty unworldly. She could've opened the door to someone, without thinking twice about it. Even if she went off alone, she could still be in danger. What if she innocently got into someone's car?' Her eyes widened.

'That van we saw yesterday, for example. Those men might've been kidnappers, not journalists. They looked pretty sus. They might've been hanging around, waiting for a chance to . . .'

'If they're kidnappers, they're pretty strange ones,' Elmo said dryly. 'Look.'

He pointed to the opposite side of the park. Sure enough, the two men in their *Miami Vice* suits and gold jewellery were getting out of their white van and sauntering towards the playground. One of them carried a notebook and the other had a camera slung around his neck. They were craning their necks in our direction. Looking for Cassandra Cass.

10

Luke gets upset

'All right, everybody,' Luke bellowed. 'Take your positions, quick smart.'

On our way back to the set, we had to push through the crowd which by now had grown quite a lot. Word really must have spread since yesterday, because more people were arriving all the time.

There were mothers and fathers with babies and older kids. Some council workers, digging drains nearby, who came over to have a look. Elderly men and women, out on their daily walk from Craigend, the old folks' home. People walking their dogs. Schoolkids on holiday. And a few teenagers—some from Raven Hill High and some I didn't recognise. Kids from the refuge, maybe?

Luke was practically tearing his hair out. 'This is getting out of control,' he groaned. 'It's starting to look more like a fair than a film shoot. Pat says that a few people have even tried to buy food from the catering van.'

Tom thought this was a huge joke. 'Have we still got that

box of The Lot?' he asked. 'I could take them around and sell
them.'

Luke scowled and started shouting orders, twice as loudly
as usual. Meanwhile, in the background, Elmo was quietly
borrowing the producer's mobile phone to ring his father.

'I want him to send a photographer down here
straightaway,' he explained. 'This'll make a great picture for
the *Pen*. A good thing too. The paper's printing tonight and
we don't really have a lead story.'

Everyone started suggesting ideas, except for me. I
concentrated on looking cool and professional. At the same
time I glanced around secretly to see whether I could spot the
two journalists. They were mingling with the crowd, stopping
every now and then to chat with some of the people, but they
didn't seem particularly interested in taking photos of us.

That was a pity. I would've liked to see my picture on the
front page.

Still, a couple of kids came over and asked for my
autograph. I signed their scrappy bits of paper, smiling sweetly,
the way Cassandra Cass always did. Now that Cassie wasn't
here, I was by far the most glamorous person on the set. The
kids knew it, even if those journalists had missed their
chance.

○

By the time the cameras started to roll again, the crowd had
doubled in size. An ice-cream van cruised up, playing

'Greensleeves' at top volume, and the assistant director raced over to it, screaming, 'Turn off the music!' Then a skinny, intense-looking girl started to hand out leaflets to the crowd. People read them and dropped them on the grass. They blew across the playground and into the shot.

Luke lost his temper. 'This is impossible,' he yelled. 'Pick up that rubbish, before I go after it with a flamethrower.'

Tom chased after one of the leaflets and pounced on it.

'Oops!' he exclaimed. 'This is the Palace movie holiday program. Mr Movies must've got tired of waiting for us to ring him back. He's given our job to somebody else.'

'Oh no!' wailed Liz predictably. 'That's *awful*!' Liz was the one who dreamed up the idea of our job agency. She protects Teen Power Inc. as fiercely as Hazel protects Cassie.

'Who cares?' I said to Liz. 'I'd rather be here in front of the cameras than over there in the crowd, handing out leaflets that nobody even wants.'

I glanced across at the skinny girl in her old, out-of-fashion clothes and watched her making one of the journalists take a leaflet. I felt a stab of sympathy. Poor thing, I thought. Imagine having to go around looking like that.

I started feeling quite depressed, but then I shook my head. There was no point in worrying about something I couldn't do anything about. Anyway, the girl would be all right. She probably didn't care about the way she looked. And at least she had a job.

The rest of the morning flew. We had lunch, and then started again. Finally, in the middle of the afternoon, Luke decided he was happy with what he had, and we were finished.

It hadn't been a bad day. I realised that even though we were finishing later than we had the day before, I wasn't as tired. I decided I was getting used to the film business. I was sorry the job was over.

At least we'd have a record of it. Nick had taken plenty of video footage, and the *Pen* photographer snapped anybody and everybody. (Including me, of course, but I wasn't particularly thrilled about it. I don't think many famous producers read the *Pen*.)

Now that the excitement was over, the crowd started to dwindle away. The two journalists had already driven off in their van. They didn't talk to any of us. It was when I saw them leave that I realised that in the excitement of the day I'd forgotten all about Cassandra Cass. I wondered whether she'd turned up at last.

The answer to that question came just as we were saying goodbye to the crew. The police arrived. Cassie still hadn't come home. And her mother had finally talked the police into doing something about it.

There were two detectives, a grey-haired, middle-aged man and a very good-looking dark-eyed woman, who wandered around asking questions like, 'When did you last see Cassandra Cass?', 'Did she seem upset yesterday?' and 'Have you noticed anything suspicious?'

We told them everything we knew, but we couldn't help

much. After ten minutes Liz looked close to tears again and actually we were all starting to feel fairly uncomfortable.

The film crew looked pretty uncomfortable as well. After all, by now it was over twenty-four hours since anyone had seen Cassie. I overheard Pat saying to Luke, 'If that poor girl really has been kidnapped, I'll never forgive myself.'

'Where is Cassie?' asked Nick, putting everybody's thoughts into words. 'Why hasn't she rung Hazel, at least? She's trying out for that drama series tomorrow. She'd never miss that. If she could help it.'

Liz shuddered. 'Don't, Nick,' she said quickly. 'I can't bear to think about it any more.'

We turned and trudged away from the playground. As we walked across the park, a trendy young woman came hurrying towards us.

'Excuse me,' she called.

We stopped while she caught up with us. She smiled around at us. 'I'm Julie Rice, from *The Morning Mail*,' she said. 'I hear Cassandra Cass is missing—perhaps kidnapped. Is that true?'

Fantastic, I thought immediately. Another chance to get my photo in the paper.

'Well, I can't tell you whether Cassie has been kidnapped,' I began eagerly. 'But . . .'

Before I could finish the sentence, Elmo pushed in front of me. His face was serious and he frowned sternly at the reporter.

'In fact, we can't tell you anything,' he said firmly. 'Sorry, but we don't know anything about it at all.'

11

Heidi

'Honestly, Elmo!' I complained as we walked up Craigend Road from the park. 'Why wouldn't you let me talk to her?'

'Because you might be putting Cassie in danger,' he said gravely. 'We don't know what's going on here, Richelle, and we don't want to make things worse for Cassie by mistake.'

'I wonder how that reporter heard about Cassie?' Liz said.

Elmo shrugged. 'She was probably in Raven Hill following up the refuge story,' he said. 'And she heard a rumour.'

'Spread by anybody who's been within twenty metres of Hazel Cass today,' Nick added. 'I bet everyone in Raven Hill knows about Cassie's disappearance by now.'

'So the reporter dropped the refuge story the minute she heard about the other. Well, I think that's really depressing,' Liz sighed. 'It's exactly what I was saying before, that . . .'

'Bad news is good news,' Tom and Sunny chorused together.

The gang split up then, and headed off in different

directions. Elmo went to help his dad on the *Pen*. (We'd be delivering the new edition tomorrow.) Liz went home and Tom and Sunny went along with her. 'We're on a mission to cheer her up,' Tom said with a grin.

Normally I have dance class on Wednesday afternoon, but there weren't any classes during the holidays, because most of the kids were away. I'd planned to go home and have a sleep, but after the filming and the crowd and the police and everything, I felt edgy and restless. So when Nick said he was going to see the man at the Palace, I decided to go with him.

❀

'Mr Movies', as Tom had called him, wasn't very nice to us. He scowled when Nick introduced himself and asked whether there were any more leaflets to give out.

'No, thanks. I'm quite happy with Heidi,' he said. 'She's given out her first lot of leaflets already and she just dropped in to collect a second batch. I know she comes from that kids' refuge, but she's reliable and she wants to work. Not like some,' he added, fixing us with an accusing stare.

I felt really embarrassed. OK, I didn't want to take the job in the first place. But I don't like being ticked off either.

Nick wasn't worried, though. He just turned on the charm and explained that he hadn't had a chance to ring back because we'd been working with Cassandra Cass. The guy looked impressed and pretty soon we were all gossiping

63

away together about Cassie and the film shoot.

'There,' Nick said triumphantly as we left. 'It pays to keep people sweet. That guy'll remember us next time he has a job. And this Heidi will have moved on by then.'

As we strolled back down Craigend Road, I spotted Heidi herself, on the other side of the road. She was standing near the pedestrian crossing beside the pub, handing out the movie ad to everybody who went by. She was good at it too. No-one got past her without taking a leaflet.

I studied her out of the corner of my eye. 'Mr Movies' certainly hadn't picked her for her looks, anyway. Her mousy hair hung round her face in oily strings. Her face was brown— not a nice bronze tan but a sort of yellowy brown, as though she'd spent too much time out in the weather.

There were dark circles under her eyes. She wasn't wearing any make-up, of course, and her clothes were really old and grotty. Her shoes were all scuffed and too big for her, and her legs were bare.

'Look at her,' I said with a shudder. Nick's eyes lit up.

'Down and out. That would make a great picture,' he muttered. 'Go across the road and walk past her, Richelle. I need you for contrast.'

'No, thanks,' I told him. I'd learnt to take orders from Luke, but I didn't have to start taking orders from Nick Kontellis as well. He was obviously beginning to fancy himself as a film director.

Nick shrugged. 'Suit yourself,' he said and he strode over to the edge of the footpath and pointed his camera at Heidi.

The homeless girl didn't even seem to notice. She just kept on handing out her leaflets, staring at the crowd with blank, hopeless eyes.

Poor kid, I thought, feeling another rush of sympathy. I bet she'd love to have a fussy, protective mother. Cassandra Cass doesn't know how lucky she is. Neither do you, said an unexpected voice in my head. I frowned. I didn't like having thoughts like that.

After a while I got bored and started looking around. 'Hey,' I exclaimed to Nick, 'there's those two guys from the park. The journalists, remember? One of them's reading the paper. Maybe he wrote a story for it, about the film shoot. We ought to buy it and find out.'

Nick didn't even bother to answer. He was too busy filming.

While I watched, the journalists got up and came out into the street. As they passed Heidi, she thrust a leaflet into their hands. Rip-off, I thought to myself. You've already given them one.

The guy with the notebook looked the girl up and down, leered and said something to her. Then he glanced at his mate with the camera, moved closer and went on talking to Heidi in a low voice.

Finally she nodded, shuffled her feet, lifted up her head and patted the back of her stringy hair. The photographer stepped back and snapped a couple of pictures.

More refuge stuff, I thought, losing interest. But just as I was turning away, I saw that the reporter had begun muttering

65

to Heidi again. I couldn't hear what he was saying, of course, but I got the impression he was making some sort of arrangement with her.

'There's something funny going on here,' Nick said suddenly, his eye still fixed to the camera's viewfinder. 'Why are those guys so interested in Heidi?'

12

Nick's theory

'They probably want to interview her,' I guessed. 'They must be doing an article on the kids' refuge as well.'

'No way. That woman Julie down at the park was from *The Morning Mail*. The *Mail* wouldn't have two lots of journalists in Raven Hill on the one day. And the other papers wouldn't want a human interest story that the *Mail* has already covered.'

'OK, then. Think of a better explanation.'

Nick frowned into the camera. 'Remember Elmo told us that some people were worried that the kids from the refuge might start dealing drugs? What if they were right? What if those guys are buying drugs from Heidi—or even supplying her with them, to sell to other kids?'

I stared at him in horror. The more I thought about the idea, the more likely it seemed. Those two men, with their slicked-back hair and flashy clothes, looked like what my dad called 'real spivs'. And Heidi—well, by the look of her she was desperate enough to do anything.

'I bet that's it,' I gasped. 'And listen, Nick, you've got the whole thing on film. We ought to go to the police straightaway.'

'Hey, cool it, Richelle,' he said, looking startled. 'It's just a theory. We don't know anything for sure. The cops'd laugh like mad if we were wrong. They'd think we were acting like stupid little kids, playing detective.'

I could see that he was right. The last thing I wanted was to make a fool of myself. But I didn't want to just forget about Heidi and the spivvy men, either. What if Nick's theory was right? It would be great to uncover a drug ring single-handed. I'd definitely get my photo in the paper then.

'Let's follow them,' I suggested with a flash of inspiration. 'If they don't do anything unusual, we'll just forget it and no-one will ever know. But if they start handing over wads of money and strange-looking parcels to each other, we'll go straight to the police, okay?'

Nick thought for a moment. 'Oh well, why not?' he grinned. Then he put his hand on my arm. 'Hey, Richelle, watch out!' he hissed. 'Heidi's looking at us.'

I glanced quickly at the opposite footpath. Nick was right. Those blank, unhappy eyes were definitely sliding in our direction. Hastily I fluffed out my hair and tucked my arm through Nick's.

'Act casual,' I said, giving him a dazzling smile. 'And you'd better stop filming, before they get suspicious.'

Heidi swung around and walked away, with the journalists close behind her. Nick stopping filming and lowered the camera. 'She must've decided that we were harmless,' he said. He dug me in the ribs. 'You're quite an actress, Richelle. Almost as good as Cassandra Cass.'

'Thanks a million,' I said, glaring at him. 'Now hurry up or we'll lose them.'

We wandered down the street, pretending to study the shop windows. There was a huge mirror in one shop, behind a display of make-up, so I peered into it, searching for the reflections of Heidi and the journalists.

'Heidi's slowing down,' I reported to Nick. 'We mustn't get too far ahead of them.'

'Right,' he said and pushed me into the doorway of the next shop. I swung back to tell him that I don't like being shoved around, but he was already pointing his video camera at me.

'Don't use all your film!' I whispered at him. 'We might need it later.'

'I'm not an idiot, Richelle,' he said coldly. 'I'm not really filming. I'm replaying the stuff I shot before. I want to check on something. Keep an eye on Heidi and the others.'

I leaned against the wall and pulled off one of my shoes, pretending to check for a blister. While I rubbed my foot, I watched Heidi and the men walking down the street. They were keeping well apart, as if they had nothing to do with each other.

'They're nearly opposite us, now,' I warned Nick. 'How much longer are you going to take?'

He let the camera drop. 'I'm no good at this,' he said, sounding annoyed at himself. 'Here, Richelle. Watch this replay and see whether you can read Heidi's lips, or the guys'. I can't pick out a single word.'

I squinted through the viewfinder and watched Heidi standing on the footpath, talking to the reporters.

'Those guys look really ridiculous, you know,' I commented. 'Don't they know that *Miami Vice* suits are seriously out? As for Heidi, I know she's living in a refuge, but even if you're down and out you can still make a bit of an effort. You don't have to look completely daggy.'

'Thanks for the fashion notes,' Nick said sarcastically. 'Now, have you picked up any of the dialogue?'

On the film Heidi had her photo taken, talked to the journalists, turned her head to look towards the video camera, then swung around and strode away, with the two men following close behind her.

I lowered the camera. 'Nick,' I said slowly.

'You got some words?' he exclaimed. 'Quick, tell me!'

'No, I can't lip-read any better than you can,' I said.

His face fell in disappointment. 'Come on, then,' he snapped. 'Stop wasting time. They're getting away.' He grabbed the video camera from me and started off up the street again. 'Hurry *up*!' he ordered over his shoulder.

'But listen, Nick!' I ran to catch him up and grabbed his arm, trying to hold him back. 'Nick, I think I'm on to something else. Could you wind the film back for me again?'

'No time,' Nick said briefly, shaking off my hand. 'They're almost out of sight. Come on, Richelle. We'll lose them!'

He pelted off again and I scuttled after him, furious. He

wouldn't listen to a word I said. All right. He'd soon find out he should have paid attention to me.

We were a long way behind Heidi and the two men by this time, and we had to jog to keep them in sight. Long distance running isn't exactly my favourite sport. I was getting hot and tired, and I was still cross with Nick. But I didn't stop. I was as interested as he was in seeing what was going to happen next.

Then Nick stopped, so suddenly that I almost ran straight into him. 'Oh no!' he murmured.

I looked over to where he was pointing. Heidi was turning off the main road, and disappearing into Ripley Avenue. But the two men weren't following. They were standing by the gutter, as if they were about to cross to our side.

The group was splitting up! What were we going to do now?

13

Playing 'Following Heidi'

The men began to cross the road. Nick grabbed me and pulled me towards him, as if he was my boyfriend saying goodbye.

'We'll have to split up too,' he muttered into my hair. 'I'll go after the guys. You follow Heidi.'

'Me? You've got to be joking. It'll be dark soon. I'm not going to play at chasing someone around Raven Hill on my own,' I protested.

Nick scowled at me. 'Listen, Richelle, this whole thing was your idea in the first place, remember.'

'No, you listen, Nick Kontellis. I've had another thought since then. Let me tell you—'

'We don't have time for your thoughts,' Nick said firmly. 'Just go! I'll meet you at the Black Cat in, say, an hour.'

He let go of me and sped after the two journalists. All right, I thought grumpily. See if I care.

I was so angry with Nick that I was within a blink of

going straight home then and there. It's amazing to think how different things would have turned out if I had. But anyway, in the end I decided I couldn't resist the chance to tell Nick off when we met at the Black Cat. And also I was quite curious to see what was going to happen next. I'd play 'Following Heidi', just as he'd asked.

I crossed the road and started down Ripley Street. Ahead of me, about half a block away, I could see my target, a daggy-looking figure moving along steadily in the fading light. I followed cautiously.

She came to a tall, plastic rubbish bin standing by a bus stop. Hardly pausing, she dumped the rest of her leaflets into it and walked on. I wasn't surprised. Obviously she'd just been using the Palace job as a cover. So much for good, responsible Heidi. 'Mr Movies', I thought, 'that'll teach you. You should have waited for Teen Power.

While I watched, she turned left into Mary Street. I went after her, trying to keep plenty of distance between us but still keeping her in sight. It wasn't easy. And the light was fading fast.

Trees hung over the footpath on Mary Street, turning it into a dark tunnel. I crept along, trying not to make any noise. There was no-one else around. Even the houses along the street were dark and silent. I found I was feeling more nervous with every step. This is a big mistake, I thought. I'm not enjoying myself at all.

At the Winston Road corner, I almost turned left and headed back up to Craigend Road and safety. I could check out the shop windows until it was time to meet Nick in the Black Cat, I thought. He'd never need to know that I'd chickened out.

Then I shook my head. Nick would find out, somehow. He always did. And then he'd give me one of those looks. Not his cool, brooding look, but his eyebrow-raised, amused, *superior* look.

I couldn't afford for Nick to get it over me like that. I had to keep playing his stupid game. So I walked right across Winston Road and into the narrower part of Mary Street where the trees were even bigger and the footpath even darker. Feeling sick to my stomach.

I'm not exactly the bravest person in the world. I admit it. I'm too sensitive for my own good, I suppose. Sunny Chan might've been able to go marching down that street in the dark without being scared. But Sunny has no imagination. I have.

And even though I was fairly sure there was no real danger in what I was doing, I wasn't a hundred per cent *certain*, was I? I've seen plenty of movies where quite clever people have fallen into traps by following up situations they thought they understood, but didn't.

What if this *was* something to do with drugs, or some other criminal activity? What if the girl ahead *knew* I was following her? What if I was being deliberately led into a trap?

That was the most frightening idea I'd come up with so far. I kept walking, but my heart was beating so loudly that I could hardly hear anything else. Then I blinked. There were

74

lights flashing in front of my eyes—bright blue lights that came closer and closer and closer.

'Don't be an idiot, Richelle,' I whispered out loud, feeling weak with relief. 'You're not seeing things. That's a police car.'

The police cruised slowly past, checking on all the houses. One of them nodded at me, and I gave him a friendly smile and tried to look as though I knew where I was going. I felt a lot safer, now I knew they were around.

At least, I felt a lot safer until I looked around for the girl and realised that she hadn't stood still and smiled at the police, like I had. No way. She'd hidden herself behind a bush, waiting till the car drove on. Now she was only just moving back out onto the footpath.

My stomach lurched, and I felt sick again. Oh no, I thought in dismay. She's definitely involved in something risky if she's trying to steer clear of the police.

I knelt down and fiddled with my shoe, keeping my head down. I needed to be extra careful now, in case I'd been seen.

Maybe I was a bit too careful. At any rate, when I looked up I found myself staring down an empty street. There was no walking figure on the footpath ahead of me. There was no sound or movement at all.

Good, I thought. I've lost her. I can go back up to Craigend Road now. Nick can't possibly blame me for this.

I expected to feel relieved, but I didn't. As a matter of fact, within about ten seconds I was feeling *furious*. Giving up on the chase of my own accord was one thing. Being given the slip was another. That was just *embarrassing*. How had that girl managed to get away from me? She thought she was so smart! But I was smarter than she was—I was sure of that.

In which case, I'd better prove it. By finding her again.

14

Scary stuff

I raced down Mary Street at top speed, looking around frantically. Then I noticed a narrow opening between two houses. I stopped and peered cautiously into the gloom. There was a little laneway there. I'd never noticed it before. It didn't even have a name, that I could see.

Obviously, she must've ducked down there. That settled one thing, at least. She wasn't leading me into a trap, after all. Instead, she was dodging through the back streets of Raven Hill, trying to make sure that no-one was following her. I wondered where on earth she was headed. It must be important, if she was going to so much trouble.

I wanted to find out what was going on, but at the same time I didn't want to go into that dark little lane. Right then I wished that I was learning tae-kwon-do, like Sunny, instead of dancing. But I wasn't learning tae-kwon-do, and I had to make a decision.

Now.

Squaring my shoulders, I strode into the side street.

Instantly there was an ear-splitting scream. It was horrible. It was weird. It wasn't human.

I might've screamed too. (I'm not sure whether I did but it would've been fair enough, right?) I certainly covered my face with my hands. Then I made a gap between my fingers and peeped out cautiously.

A fluffy ginger cat was scrambling up the side of a paling fence at the speed of light. It perched on top of one of the fence posts, flicked its ears indignantly at me and started to lick the tip of its tail.

Not a human scream, I realised. A cat scream. I'd obviously stepped on its tail.

'Sorry, cat,' I whispered. And then I laughed. I'm hysterical, I thought. Talking to a cat.

The cat gave me a cool, brooding look, like a fluffy ginger version of Nick Kontellis. I left it sitting there and hurried on down the lane. It curved gently for a while and then straightened out, running along between the backs of two rows of little old houses. Once I got to the straight bit I could see a small figure disappearing into the distance. Yes! The 'Following Heidi' game was on again.

I ran along on tiptoes, starting to feel nervous all over again. My knees started trembling. I thought I knew Raven Hill pretty well, but I'd never been in this part of it before.

I stopped. I can't go on, I thought, as the gloom of the lane closed in on me. I'm not a brave person. I'm not Sunny Chan. I don't like places that I don't know. I'll have to stop this. I'll have to turn back.

But I knew I *couldn't* turn back. Not after getting this far.
I hesitated. I couldn't go on, and I couldn't turn back. What
was I going to do?

Then I had a thought. I wasn't a brave person . . . but I
was a good actress. Nick had said so himself. Maybe I could
put on an act. For anyone who was watching—and for myself.

So I decided to pretend I was looking for a lost kitten. (I
got the idea from the ginger cat, of course.) I began jogging
along past the old houses with their high paling fences,
hissing, 'Here, puss. Here, puss, puss.'

It sounds funny, but after a while I really got into it. I
started to feel seriously worried about my poor lost pet.

And it worked. By the time I got to the end of the lane, I
wasn't scared at all. Just cross, because I couldn't see anyone
ahead of me.

In fact, I must have been feeling really calm, because
when there was a thump and bang behind me, I didn't faint
on the spot. I didn't even jump. I just turned around and
smiled at the old woman who was wheeling her rubbish bin
out through her back gate.

'Hi,' I said brightly. Then, in case she'd heard me calling
'Puss, puss', I added, 'Have you seen a little Siamese kitten?'
(My aunt has a Siamese cat. It's really elegant. If I had to have
a pet, I'd have one of those.)

'No, I'm afraid not, dear,' the old woman said, full of
sympathy.

'Well, have you seen my friend, by any chance?' I asked,
crossing my fingers behind my back. 'She was helping me

look, and now I've lost her too.'

'I heard someone walking down the lane past the fence here a few minutes ago,' the old woman said. 'That might have been her. If it was, she's probably gone on across the road to Raven Hill Park. I do hope your little cat hasn't got lost there, dear.'

'I'll go and see,' I said, beaming at her. 'Thanks very, very much.'

It was good to know where to go, but I must say it was a bit annoying to find that I'd ended up at the park again. I could've just walked straight down Craigend Road instead of creeping around little back streets and scaring myself stupid.

Funnily enough, though, I didn't really mind. If I'd just walked back down the main street to the park, I wouldn't have found out how to act brave. Nick Kontellis probably wouldn't have been impressed by my great discovery. He'd obviously expected me to play 'Following Heidi' without thinking twice about it. But I was impressed by myself. Very impressed.

I came out of the lane into Park Road! I groaned at myself. In my travels and fright I'd lost all my sense of direction. Besides, it had been very dim in the lane. I'd had no idea where I was.

By now the sun had nearly set behind Raven Hill Park. The sky was dark with rain clouds shot with dull, angry-looking pink, and shadows were beginning to gather underneath the trees.

I was braver than before, but I wasn't stupid. It was one

thing to follow someone through the back streets in the late afternoon. It was another thing to follow her through the park after dark. I wasn't going in there on my own. No way.

Still, there was no harm in crossing the road to take a closer look, so I did.

There was a huge, spreading fig tree near the edge of the park just here, with an old white van parked beside it. I don't know much about cars, but I had a feeling that I'd seen this one before. One of the film crew's vans, maybe? No, it was too battered-looking for that.

I went closer, hoping to find some sort of clue. The back doors of the van were open. I sidled up to the nearest door and peered around it.

Then someone grabbed me by the shoulder.

15

No place
to hide

I nearly jumped out of my skin. And I bet Sunny Chan
would've too, if someone had grabbed hold of her near a dark,
lonely park. Anybody would, believe me.

I whirled around and stared straight into a pair of
piercing, dark eyes. Then, just as I opened my mouth to
scream for help, I realised that they were familiar.

They were Nick Kontellis's eyes.

I shut my mouth and hung on to the van door to steady
myself. Nick put his finger to his lips to warn me to be quiet.
Then he patted my shoulder awkwardly. For once, he looked
almost apologetic.

'Sorry. I didn't mean to scare you, Richelle,' he
whispered. 'I just thought I ought to let you know I was here.'

'You could've picked a better way,' I breathed, still
shaking. Then I pulled myself together. 'Why are we
whispering?' I demanded. 'And why are you here, anyway?

You were supposed to be following the two men.'

'I did,' hissed Nick. 'They're here. Don't you recognise their van?'

Of course. That was where I'd seen the van before.

'Where are they?' I craned my neck, but couldn't see over the van doors.

'Underneath the fig tree, talking to Heidi. The three of them obviously wanted to have a secret meeting. The guys picked up the van and came straight down Craigend Road. She came to the park through the back streets so no-one would suspect. If we can get a bit closer, we might be able to hear what they're saying. What do you reckon?'

'Why not?' I shrugged, as if I had nerves of steel. 'We've come this far.'

I felt better now that Nick was with me. And besides, now that I knew that a secret meeting had been set up, I was even more determined to find out exactly what was up.

Nick and I crept back along the side of the van and peered cautiously around the headlight. The two journalists were propped against the tree and the girl was pacing up and down as she talked to them. I couldn't hear her. She talked too quietly for that. But I heard a few words of what the men were saying in reply.

'Great stuff,' the guy with the camera was commenting. And later the other guy said something that ended, '. . . tell your story to the world.' After that, the photographer said something about 'our office'.

Oh, yes, I thought. So that's how it is. I thought so.

Just then there was a rumble of thunder, and rain started spitting down. I tuned out of the conversation under the fig tree and started to worry about my hair. I try to stay out of the rain. It makes my hair go into these tight frizzy curls.

Time to go home, I decided. I was tugging at Nick's jacket when the photographer pushed himself away from the tree and started walking towards the van.

Towards us.

Without stopping to think, I spun around and bolted for the back of the van, hiding between the open doors. Nick pelted after me. We clutched at each other and listened while the photographer opened the driver's door. My heart was beating fast again. I didn't want to be found here, listening in to these people. The situation could get really nasty.

'He didn't see us,' Nick whispered, sounding relieved. 'I'll check on the other guy.'

He edged over to the far side of the van and looked around the door. I followed him, hanging onto the back of his jacket. Oh, no! The other two were leaving the fig tree now, and coming our way. Any minute now we were going to be found out!

I glanced around desperately. Empty park, empty street. The men would certainly see us if we made a run for it. Then they'd probably chase after us. And almost certainly catch us, too. Well, catch me, anyway. But there was nowhere to hide.

The back of the van! I looked through the open doors. It was all enclosed, like a small room. And empty, except for a toolbox, a spare tyre and a crumpled old tarpaulin.

I elbowed Nick and pointed. Then, without making a sound, I scrambled into the van and dived under the tarpaulin, hauling it over me. A few seconds later Nick joined me.

'I'm surprised at you, Richelle,' he whispered. 'I thought you'd rather be caught than get your clothes dirty.'

That's typical of Nick. He always has to show you how cool he is, even in a crisis. (*Especially* in a crisis.) I peeped out from under the tarpaulin, tucked it around me more securely and prodded him in the back.

'Pull your foot in,' I hissed. 'It's still sticking out.'

Nick wriggled around and adjusted the heavy cloth. Just in time, too, because just at that moment someone climbed into the back of the van with us! We both lay rigid, hardly daring to breathe.

The doors slammed shut. The engine revved. Nick's hand gripped my arm. Oh wow, I thought. We've done it now.

16

The long,
long ride

The van pulled away from the kerb and accelerated sharply. There was a thump and an irritated exclamation from the person in the back with us.

'It's Heidi!' Nick's voice breathed in my ear. 'Don't move!'

As if I would. I wondered where we were going to end up, but I wasn't all that worried. The guys' office couldn't possibly be very far from here. Once they parked the van, we could just slip out and I had enough money to catch a taxi home.

And before we went home, we might even find out the answers to some interesting questions. I hadn't heard enough to satisfy me yet. What exactly was going on here? Why the very secret meeting? Was the promise to 'tell the story to the world' a promise, or a threat?

I thought I knew a few of the answers, but I wasn't absolutely sure. One thing was certain, though. Even if I didn't manage to capture a drug ring single-handed, this was still going to make a great story. I could hardly wait to tell the rest of the Teen Power gang.

The van kept stopping and starting as it threaded its way through the traffic. I lifted the tarpaulin very carefully and peeped out. It was dark, because there were no windows, just slits near the roof to let in air. But I could see the figure of the girl sitting quietly on the spare tyre, smiling to herself.

I watched her for a bit and then I watched the wall of the van. Lights from outside were flashing in through the ventilation slits, so I amused myself by counting the traffic lights. Two red lights . . . one green light . . . one red light . . . another . . .

The rain was pouring down full pelt. It drummed on the roof of the van, drowning out any other sounds. Like a heavy metal band, I thought. After a while I got sick of it. I wanted it to stop—and it did, for a moment, but then it started again. We must've gone under a bridge or an overpass, I suppose.

After about ten minutes we sped up. The road was smooth. The traffic lights had stopped flashing into the slits in the wall. The rain went on pounding on the roof. I was beginning to feel pretty bored. (I hadn't realised that adventures could be boring, as well as scary.) The ride was taking much longer than I'd expected. The van was terribly stuffy. And there wasn't much to look at through the gap in the tarpaulin.

The figure sitting on the spare tyre had begun shifting

uncomfortably. She was obviously getting bored, too.

Suddenly the van slowed right down. We crawled along for ages, stopping and starting. Blue and red lights flashed across the wall in a weird pattern. I shut my eyes. I could hardly breathe. I didn't know how much more of this I could stand.

○

We were off again, zooming even faster than before.

I heard Nick muttering under his breath beside me. He was obviously wondering what was going on. And so was I. I'd assumed we were heading for a city office, but we'd already gone much further than that.

'What's Heidi doing?' Nick breathed. He was worse off than me. He couldn't see a thing except the van doors.

'Nothing,' I whispered in reply. 'But Nick . . .'

Then suddenly the girl did do something. She clicked her tongue in exasperation and stood up, banging on the wall that separated the back of the van from the front. 'Hey!' she shrilled. 'Hey!'

There was no response. She tried banging and shouting a couple of times and then sulkily sat down on the tyre again.

No wonder she was bored and uncomfortable. By now we'd been travelling for forty long minutes! I was sure of that, because I was beginning to feel car-sick.

That was a real worry. I could hardly call out, 'Hey, could you stop the van for a minute, so I can be sick?' and then go back and hide under the tarpaulin again afterwards. And if I threw up in the back of the van, we'd be found out for sure. I mean, there's no way that you can throw up quietly.

And Nick was with me. The last thing I needed was to throw up in front of Nick. I think the idea of that scared me worse than anything.

I swallowed hard. Then the van swerved to the left and went over a huge bump and I gasped out loud. Nick kicked my ankle sharply. Oh no, I thought in panic. He obviously heard me. What if she did too?

I lay there, stiff with terror, waiting for the tarpaulin to be whisked off me. But nothing happened and gradually I started to relax. The rain was still beating down on the roof of the van. It must have masked any sound I made.

The ride had become very uncomfortable now. We chugged up one steep hill and plunged down another. Then the van rocked from side to side as it swung around a series of sharp bends and corners. I could feel every bump in the road—and there were a lot of bumps. At least I hadn't thrown up, though.

Finally the van went down another steep hill, and slowed right down. I was feeling awful. I breathed deeply. The air in the van was very stuffy, but there was a faint smell coming in through the slits in the wall. A nice, fresh smell. Could we be in the country?

We veered abruptly to the right. Then we jolted over an even bumpier bit of road for five minutes. Then we stopped.

It was a tremendous relief to be free of the shuddering of

the engine. Nick and I lay very still. We heard footsteps, and then a bang, as the back doors were opened.

The rain was still teeming down. Fresh air streamed into the van. I gulped it in through the gap in the tarpaulin. It smelt incredibly fresh and tangy. It was wonderful.

'Time to get out, sweetheart!' grinned the man at the back doors.

'About time!' the girl snapped, scrambling towards him, out of my sight. There was a pause. Then her voice came again. 'Where—where are we?' she stammered. The words were almost drowned out by the drumming of the rain, but even so I could hear the sudden doubt and fear in them.

Then she screamed.

I heard Nick gasp. I jerked up my head and twisted around so I could see what he was seeing through the van doors. An icy hand seemed to clutch at my heart. Darkness, trees, driving rain, the high roof of an old house. Two shadowy figures, holding the girl's arms.

Two shadowy figures, dragging the girl across the sodden grass. She was fighting, struggling and screaming.

'No!' she was screaming. 'No! Let me go!'

17

Terror!

She screamed again, wrenching her body left and right, trying to get away. I heard one of the men snarl. I saw him wrestle with her, wrapping a rope around her wrists while the other man stuffed a gag into her mouth. She went limp and the first man started to push her towards the house again.

Nick had thrown off the tarpaulin. We sat up, side by side, clutching each other. My head was whirling. I couldn't believe what I was seeing. My teeth started to chatter.

Suddenly Nick flung himself across me and pushed me down onto the floor, dragging the tarpaulin over us again.

One of the men had come back. There was a crash as the van doors slammed shut. Then the engine roared into life again. The van reversed sharply, turned and sped off, with us imprisoned inside.

We banged and jolted over the bumps. 'Nick!' I whispered, through my chattering teeth. 'Nick, what are we going to do?'

Nick shifted position and lifted his arm. I could see the luminous dial of his watch glowing in the dark. This is no time to start worrying about the time! I thought wildly. What's he *doing*?

'Nick, we've got to save her,' I cried. 'We've got to *do* something! Don't you realise, she's—'

Before I could finish, he twisted around and clamped his hand over my mouth. 'Don't make another sound,' he hissed. 'Don't you understand the danger we're in?'

Of course I did. But that girl back at the house was ten times worse off. Those creepy guys . . . I shuddered, digging my nails into my palms. We had to help her. But what could we do? We couldn't get out of the speeding van. And even if we could, we had no idea of where we were. I couldn't even begin to think of a plan.

The van was going even faster than before, now. It belted around the bends, tossing us from side to side. I hit my elbow against the wall and bit my lip to stop myself from groaning. Already I ached all over.

Nick was fiddling with his video camera, putting in a new video cassette. Then he pointed the camera at the wall of the van. Was he crazy? It was dark, and there was nothing to film in here.

'What are you doing?' I demanded and he shushed me again.

'Keep quiet and listen, Richelle,' he whispered. 'We have to try and work out where we are. That's the only thing we can do for Heidi right now.'

I had to admit he was right. But I didn't think the camera would be much help. I couldn't see a thing.

Still, I could hear things, like the rush of the rain and the sound of branches scraping the roof of the van. And I could feel things too. As we rattled along, I tried to memorise every bump and jolt and bend in the road. It wasn't easy.

Especially as all the time I kept getting pictures in my mind of what I'd seen and heard through the van doors back at the old house. That desperate struggle in the driving rain. That terrible screaming, and the snarling of the man as he wrestled with his victim, and tied her wrists. I kept remembering how small and skinny she was, how alone and unprotected. How helpless.

I dug my nails into my palms again. I'd thought I had everything worked out. I thought I was so smart. I'd treated this whole thing as a game. A scary game, but a game all the same. And I'd been completely wrong.

If only I'd made Nick listen to me. If only we hadn't hidden in the van. If only we'd confronted those guys, while we were still in the park. Then they'd never have dared to follow through with their plan.

In other words, it was all my fault. I wasn't going to have a great story to tell about this, after all. Liz and Sunny and the others weren't going to be impressed. Instead, everyone would probably think I'd been very stupid. Selfish and irresponsible. I could practically hear Elmo's voice, saying those exact words, and I squirmed under the tarpaulin.

Sometimes it can be a problem if you worry too much about what other people think of you. But sometimes it can be a big help. For most of our return trip, I felt sicker than I've ever felt in my entire life. Only one thing stopped me from throwing up—the thought of Nick Kontellis's face, if I spewed all over him. He would've looked so disgusted. I couldn't have handled that.

So I clamped my mouth shut and tried to count traffic lights, while my stomach churned and heaved. Just as I was deciding that I didn't care what Nick thought of me after all, the van stopped. Another traffic light, I thought gloomily, but then the engine stopped as well.

The driver's door slammed. And then there was silence.

Minutes ticked by. We heard a few cars zipping past. A siren in the distance. Some people talking as they walked along the street.

'He's gone,' Nick said, flinging off the tarpaulin.

We hurtled for the doors, and wrestled them open. We fell out onto the road. I drank in the fresh air greedily. Rain was still falling, wetting my face and clothes and hair. But I didn't care. It was a minute at least before I even looked up to see where we were. And when I did, I thought I must be dreaming.

We were back beside the fig tree, at Raven Hill Park.

'He's left the doors unlocked,' said Nick. 'He must be dumping the van. It's probably stolen.'

I looked around nervously. There was no sign of the man at all. But over on Craigend Road I saw something that made my heart leap.

'Nick!' I squeaked excitedly. 'Over there! Do you see what I see?'

A police car was cruising along the edge of the park, just

like the one I'd seen driving up Mary Street earlier on. We raced towards it, waving our arms and shouting. The car slowed to a halt and a spotty policeman looked enquiringly out the window at us.

We must have looked very weird. Filthy and wild-eyed, with our hair everywhere. His enquiring look quickly changed to a grave one. 'What's happened?' he asked quickly. 'Something wrong?'

I stared at him for a second, speechless, then I burst into tears.

○

I went on crying at the police station. I couldn't stop, and they made me lie down on this couch. It was so embarrassing, but I couldn't help it. The whole thing had been such a terrible shock.

The woman detective we'd seen at the park was there. Her name was Angela Maroni. She'd rung our parents when we first arrived, and convinced them that we were safe. She said the police needed to talk to us for a while, but that they'd bring us home as soon as possible.

Anyway, while I went through half a box of tissues, Nick poured out the story. He told them how we'd noticed Heidi and followed her and hidden in the van. When he told them how the guys had grabbed her, I started to cry even harder.

'It's so *awful*,' I sobbed. 'I feel so sorry for her. She thought she was being so clever and now she's in terrible trouble.'

Angela made soothing noises at me and then Dan Reilly, the other detective, picked up the phone on his desk and punched in some numbers. He waited, tapping his fingers on his desk.

'Reilly here, from Raven Hill,' he began, when the phone was answered at the other end. 'We need some assistance. An abduction. Young woman.'

There was a quacking sound from the phone. Dan listened to it with a frown. He obviously didn't agree with what the quacking person was saying.

'No, no,' he snapped when he got the chance. 'Will you listen? I'm not talking about Cassandra Cass. If that's an abduction, I'm the Queen's great uncle. It's a publicity stunt, I'm telling you. She left the house perfectly willingly. We all saw the place. We all know that. Cassandra Cass hasn't been kidnapped.'

Straightaway my tears dried up, as if by magic. I jumped up and ran over to him.

'Yes, she has,' I told him urgently. 'She has!'

Nick rolled his eyes and looked embarrassed. 'Richelle . . .' he muttered, trying to pull me back.

Dan put his hand across the phone. 'What do you mean?' he asked, staring at me. 'How do you know?'

'Because we saw it,' I burst out. 'Because Heidi—she's not Heidi at all. She's Cassandra Cass.'

18

I explain
a few things

Everybody stared at me. Dan, Angela, and Nick. Dan recovered first.

'I'll get back to you,' he said into the phone. He slammed down the receiver and turned back to me. 'Richelle, are you sure about this?'

I nodded, swallowing. 'Cassie disguised herself,' I said. 'I think she was trying to prove she could really act. Be someone other than those pretty, sweet girls she always plays. She looked really different as Heidi. I didn't recognise her at first. But as soon as I saw her through Nick's video camera, I knew.'

'But—but why didn't you *tell* me?' exploded Nick.

'I tried to a couple of times but you wouldn't listen,' I said, sniffling into a tissue.

'Well I'm listening now. Tell me!'

'I saw her on videotape, when you asked me to try to read her lips, and I recognised her,' I said. 'She looks different on film. Like Elmo said, the camera loves her. I first realised when Heidi patted the back of her hair, like Cassie always does, when she was having her photograph taken. And when she walked away I recognised the walk. Cassie's walk.'

Dan looked at Nick. 'Seems funny you didn't recognise the girl, if this is true,' he rumbled.

Nick looked confused. A first for Nick. I almost smiled through my tears.

'If you saw her you'd understand,' I said to Dan. 'As Heidi, Cassie looked—really down and out. Really daggy.'

'She has this brown, stringy hair,' mumbled Nick.

'She's wearing a wig,' I said. 'She probably pinched it from the make-up van before she left. Remember Pat saying that everything was in a mess?'

'And her eyes, and even her skin. They're . . .'

'She's taken out her tinted contact lenses,' I reminded him. 'And I'd say that before she left home she used the fake tan she usually uses on her legs and arms to make her face brown. She put shadows under her eyes with eyeshadow.'

'The clothes . . .' faltered Nick.

'Were from the op shop that Liz told her about, I'll bet.' I felt almost smug as I saw that he was finally convinced.

'And then she went to the Palace and took our job,' Nick said bitterly. 'What a smart operator.'

'Not so smart,' I told him. 'Smart in some ways, completely stupid in others. She believed that those guys were real journalists—but they weren't. They'd been staking her out, waiting for a chance to snatch her.' I bit my lip.

'She made it easy for them, by changing her looks and dropping out of sight,' I went on. 'Then she played right into their hands. She told them who she was. Probably in the park, on the second day of filming. We saw her giving one of them a leaflet, remember? I think she offered them the story of her two days living another life.'

'Looking for publicity, because of that audition tomorrow,' murmured Nick.

'That's right,' I said. 'She arranged a secret meeting with them. They said they'd do an interview with her at the newspaper office. So she got into the van without a struggle. She helped with her own kidnapping. If you ask me, she isn't very smart at all.'

Dan Reilly picked up the phone again, punched numbers. 'Reilly from Raven Hill again,' he barked. 'Look, get some people over here. Fast. Seems Cassandra Cass is the girl we're talking about all right. Yes . . . What? What? When? Right!'

He crashed the receiver down and swung around to us.

'Maroni,' he barked. 'Hazel Cass has just been contacted by the kidnappers with a ransom demand. Half a million dollars. They let her speak to her daughter. They said they'd ring again at eleven, tell her where to leave the money and let her speak to Cassie again. And that's it. No more contact. If she doesn't pay up, she never sees her daughter again.'

Nick and I looked at each other, horrified. 'Can she get the money?' I quavered.

Angela Maroni tightened her lips. 'The money's not the

problem,' she said, grimly. She glanced at the other detective.
'In these cases,' she went on, 'whatever the kidnappers say,
there's no guarantee that the victim will be returned
unharmed. In fact, there's a very great risk that . . .'

My heart felt as though it was being squeezed.

'You mean they might hurt Cassie anyway?' I whispered.

Dan Reilly cleared his throat and stood up. 'Not if we
catch them first,' he growled.

'She's alive now, at any rate,' said Angela. 'And will be at
least until eleven tonight. That gives us just over three hours
to find her. And that's where you kids come in.'

O

They took us into one of the interview rooms and hooked
Nick's camera up to the TV there. Then we watched the
recording of Cassie/Heidi talking to the two men on Craigend
Road. Angela turned out to be a better lip-reader than either
Nick or me.

'Cassie's saying, "Seen enough?",' she told us, staring
intently into the screen. 'Now one of the guys is saying,
"You're magic". And the other guy says—hmm, let me play it
back again. Yes, I've got it. He's saying, "I'll take two pictures
now, then we'll meet you at the park and set up the
interview".'

'It was a set up, all right,' Dan said, nodding at me. 'The
poor kid fell straight into it.'

'We can get prints off the video, to help us identify the

men,' said Angela. 'But that'll take time. More time than we've got. We'll have to hope there are some clues in the van.'

At that moment the spotty constable knocked and came into the room, looking worried.

'Well?' demanded Angela eagerly.

'It's not so good, sir,' he said, shaking his head at her. 'The numberplates on the van are fake. The van itself was probably stolen, and the plates changed, but we haven't traced it yet. Plus there's nothing in the front of the van to give us any clues about the driver or the passenger. Forensic will be able to tell us a bit more, of course—'

'Not in three hours, they won't!' exclaimed Angela.

Three hours. Three hours. The words beat in my head. The seconds hand on the big wall clock ticked around remorselessly. I thought of Hazel Cass, waiting helplessly at home by the phone. Of Cassie, terrified, in that awful old house. Three hours . . .

19

It's up to us

'All right,' Dan said firmly. 'Then it's up to us. What's on the other cassette, Nick?'

'The film I shot while the van was driving us back to the city,' Nick said, sticking his hands in his pockets and trying to be cool. 'You won't be able to see much on it, of course. It was dark. But there were changes of light through the ventilation slits. I just thought . . .'

'Nick, you're a genius!' Angela exclaimed.

I'd often wondered what it would take to make Nick Kontellis blush and now I know. You just have to tell him he's a genius, in front of four other people. (Of course, it helps if you're a stunning policewoman with curly dark hair and huge dark eyes, as well.)

After that, they gave us some sandwiches and fruit juice. We were both starving. And while we were still eating, we got down to work.

Nick and I had to describe our trip from Raven Hill Park to the old house and back, including every single detail we could think of. Every bump. Every jolt. Every corner. Every traffic light.

At the same time, Dan and Angela and a couple of other detectives, experts from city headquarters who came in soon after we'd started, looked at Nick's video. They watched it forwards and backwards, fast and frame by frame, and tried to match it to our description.

Sounds simple? Well, it wasn't. We watched that video over and over, making notes and timing it with a stopwatch. It took forever. We had to go through our story over and over and over again too. It was exhausting, but it was worth it, because every time we told it we remembered a bit more.

I remembered the overpass where the rain had seemed to stop for a few seconds. Nick remembered every traffic light we'd passed through on our way back.

Every time we remembered something new, Angela would hover over the street map, trying to place it. 'Damn, there are two overpasses near Raven Hill Park,' she would tell us. Or else she'd shout, 'Got it!' and stick another marking pin in the map.

And every time she stuck another pin in the map, we had to check the timing of the journey all over again. Nick was terrific there. He'd used his watch to time the return journey (forty-five minutes) and, of course, his video was absolutely vital.

Because of the video you could tell how long we'd spent travelling through the dark hilly bits, how long we'd spent travelling along the smooth straight road and how long we'd spent jolting from traffic light to traffic light in the city.

It was like doing a jigsaw puzzle, only a hundred times as hard. We had to identify all the lights and sounds on the video. We had to remember all the details we'd noticed along the way and get them in the right order. And then we had to work out where all of this fitted on the timeline.

'The smooth straight stretch of road with no traffic lights is obviously a freeway,' said one of the city detectives.

'Yes, and I bet it was the F4,' Dan said excitedly. 'That fits with the description of the trip from Raven Hill Park. And the kids said the van slowed to a crawl for quite a long while—well, there was a big accident on the F4 tonight that held up the traffic for about fifteen minutes!'

'Yes,' exclaimed Angela. 'Now, where did they turn off the freeway?'

'Oh, I know that,' I said. They all turned to stare at me.

I felt myself blushing. 'I started to get car-sick just before the van went off onto those hilly roads,' I mumbled. 'And I always get car-sick exactly forty minutes after I set out, whether the car's travelling fast or slow.'

The city experts grimaced at one another.

But Angela flung her arms into the air. 'Richelle, you're a genius!' she shouted. 'That's *exactly* what we needed to know.'

I glanced triumphantly at Nick. That'll show him, I thought. He's not the only genius in this team. (Although I must say I wished I could've done something a bit more spectacular than just getting car-sick.)

The police bent over the map again, muttering about car speeds, estimating times. Finally they stuck another pin into the map.

'Right. We've made a start,' said the head expert. 'But time's running out fast. It's ten o'clock already. We can't wait here any longer. We'll have to drive along the same route, take the turn-off we think might be the right one, and see where we go from there.'

Angela found some jackets for Nick and me and we bundled into a car—an unmarked police car because we didn't want the kidnappers to spot us.

The experts followed behind us in a second car, with some more police in uniform.

We drove to Raven Hill Park and Angela looked at her watch. 'Here goes,' she said. 'Cross your fingers.'

Nick closed his eyes and listened to the sounds around us. We wove through the streets for about ten minutes and then shot out onto the F4 right on schedule. We drove along the smooth surface for about another fifteen minutes. No delays this time. Then a sign loomed up ahead.

Angela looked at her watch and her map and said, 'Now! If Richelle's right, this should be the turn off.'

I stared anxiously out of the window as Dan swung the car off into the freeway exit ramp. Was this really the place?

Then there was a sickening jolt as the car hit a hole in the road. 'Oh wow,' I yelled, remembering the last time we'd driven over this bump. 'Yes! This is it! It really is it!'

Nick leaned over and punched me on the arm.

'You did it, Richelle,' he shouted. 'You and your queasy stomach!'

'Hold the celebrations,' Angela said. 'We're not there yet. The hardest part's still to come. From here on, we're driving blind.'

20

Left or right?

'Would you believe, I'm not car-sick this time?' I commented. 'Maybe I've been cured.'

'I doubt it,' Nick said in his most superior voice. 'You've forgotten, Richelle. Last time we had that fifteen minute delay on the F4, so we'd been travelling for forty minutes by the time we got to the turn-off. This time we've only been going . . .'

'OK,' I snapped. 'I can work it out for myself, thanks. I just forgot about the delay for a minute, that's all.'

Then I stopped arguing, because Nick had closed his eyes again. It's hard to argue with someone who can't even see you. The car jolted along past long lines of shadowy trees and came to a fork in the road.

'Where now?' Dan asked and Nick said confidently, 'We turned left here.'

What a memory, I thought. How does he do it?

During the next ten minutes, Nick did his memory trick three more times, which was lucky for us because the hills turned out to be full of small dirt tracks, leading off in all directions. It would've taken hours to explore every single track, but Nick and his amazing memory were able to lead us through the maze.

Finally the car plunged down a steep hill. At the bottom we could see that the road forked. 'Which way next?' Angela said eagerly.

Nick hesitated. 'I'm not sure,' he muttered. 'I'm sorry, but this time I really can't remember.'

'Never mind,' Dan told him. 'You've done brilliantly up until now. We'll just have to do some exploring. We can't be far from the house now.'

'No, we're not,' I said in a small voice. 'We're exactly five minutes away.'

Angela twisted around to look at me. 'How do you know, Richelle?' she said and then she chuckled. 'Oops, I shouldn't have needed to ask. Your face looks positively green. You're feeling sick, aren't you? Why don't you roll the window down and let in some fresh air?'

I hung out of the window, breathing deeply. My stomach was churning and there was a sour taste at the back of my mouth. There was an odd sensation at the back of my memory too.

'Hey, I think I recognise something,' I said in surprise. 'Can you drive on a bit further, Dan?'

The car rolled down the slope and I sniffed the air again. 'Yes,' I said positively. 'It's that smell. I remember it. We veered to the right, just past here. And at the house—the smell's even stronger.'

Angela gave a shout of triumph. 'We've got it,' she announced, banging the map. 'The right-hand road goes down to the river. You smelt the *river*, Richelle.'

We took the right-hand road, which was more like a narrow dirt track, full of all the bumps I remembered. Dan turned off the headlights and slowed right down. The car crawled along, while Angela looked at her watch.

'Dan, it's five to eleven,' she said anxiously. 'They'll be ringing Hazel Cass soon. After that, they won't need Cassie any more. She'll just be a burden to them. We have to hurry.'

It was dark without the headlights, and very spooky. I peered into the night, searching desperately for some sign of the kidnappers' hideout. Suddenly, Nick and I clutched each other.

'There it is,' we said in unison. 'There's the house.'

Darkness, trees, the high roof of an old house . . . as I stared at it, I heard the echo of Cassie's scream as the kidnappers grabbed her. What was she feeling now? Was she still hoping that someone might come to rescue her? Or had she given up hope?

Dan swung the car across the road, blocking it completely. He and Angela got out and waited until the second car arrived. The police talked together briefly in low voices and then Angela came over to us.

'We're going in now,' she said, her dark eyes glittering in the dim light. 'You stay here, out of sight. They could be armed. Now, no silly stuff. Understand?'

'Of course we do,' Nick said crossly. 'We're not little kids, you know.'

'Neither you are,' she said with a grin. 'Sorry.'

She melted away into the shadows. Nick and I sat there in silence for what seemed like ages, straining our ears for any sound. Every time a twig cracked or a breeze rustled the bushes, I almost jumped out of my skin with fright.

Finally Nick whispered, 'Listen, Angela only told us to wait here. She didn't say we actually had to stay inside the car, did she?'

I didn't have to be asked twice. We scrambled out of the car as quietly as we could and stood leaning against it. I sniffed the smell of the river. Now I thought I could almost hear it stirring and rippling behind the trees. But there wasn't anything else to hear.

I found I was holding my breath, and tried to make myself relax.

Then suddenly everything happened at once. Doors slammed. Voices shouted. There was a thump, and a crash. Then there was a single gunshot. Seconds later the front door of the house slammed open and a dark figure hurtled out.

'Who's that?' hissed Nick. 'What's he doing?'

I took a quick glance at the man who was now running straight for us. His hair flopped over his face. He had no moustache. He was wearing jeans and a checked shirt . . .

But there was no mistaking those mean little eyes.

'It's one of them!' I yelled. 'He's going to take the car and get away!'

'Keep back,' ordered Nick. And then he jumped out from the shadow of the car and stuck his leg out in front of the running figure. The man tripped, but didn't fall. He whirled round and flung out his arm, knocking Nick sideways.

Then he pulled up, and saw me. For a few seconds we stared at each other. And in those few seconds I could see the thoughts flashing behind those cold eyes. Another girl to grab. A hostage. His passport out of here.

21

Richelle the heroine

It's strange, the things that go through your mind in a crisis. While I stood there facing the guy, I found myself wishing for the second time that I'd signed up for tae-kwon-do, instead of dance classes.

Then, almost without thinking about it, I swung up my right leg, in the most perfect high kick that I've ever done. There was a loud crack as my foot connected with the man's jaw. He rolled up his eyes in a look of astonishment—and fell flat on his back.

Nick raced over and sat on his chest. 'I never realised that dancing could be lethal, Richelle,' he said faintly. 'What should we do now?'

'I suppose we wait for the police, like Angela told us to do,' I said calmly. 'I wonder why they're taking so long. We dealt with our kidnapper in about three minutes flat.'

Nick looked at me. 'Richelle,' he said. 'You're amazing.'

'Are you sure you're all right?' I asked Cassandra Cass as we rocked from side to side in the back of the police car on the way back to Raven Hill. She seemed amazingly calm, considering all she'd been through.

She shrugged. 'I'm really tired and I twisted my ankle a bit back there, but that's all. Don't worry, Richelle. It won't wreck my chances tomorrow.'

Nick's jaw dropped. 'Cassie!' he exclaimed. 'You're not planning to go to that casting session, after all this, are you?'

'Of course I am,' Cassie said with a steely glint in her blue eyes. 'I went to all this trouble to change my image. I'm not going to wimp out now.'

'How did you dream up that crazy idea, Cassie?' asked Angela dryly, from the front seat.

'It was the kids,' Cassie yawned. 'Teen Power. The little red-headed one, Elmo, kept talking about this refuge for homeless kids. And then I remembered how Anna Wheat had talked to a bunch of homeless kids when she was preparing for her role in *On the Streets*. So I decided to go one better and actually live as a homeless kid for a day.'

She sighed with satisfaction. 'And I did it, too,' she said. 'Mind you, I'm pretty sick of Heidi now. I'm dying for a nice hot shower and my soft bed.'

'Wouldn't it have been a good idea to let your mother in on the plan?' asked Angela, still in that dry voice.

Cassie looked around with wide-open, innocent blue eyes. 'Oh, I couldn't have done that,' she said. 'She'd never have let me do it.'

113

For her, that seemed to be that.

'Weren't you scared, when the kidnappers had you?' I asked.

She hesitated for a moment. 'I don't know whether you'll understand this, Richelle, but, well, of course I was scared. Really scared. But I knew that I had to stay cool, in case I had a chance to escape. So, I remembered that I was an actress and I decided to act as though I was brave. And I did. It helped a lot. Does that make sense to you?'

I nodded. Of course it made sense. I'd done exactly the same thing myself while I was following her through the back streets of Raven Hill. I hadn't felt brave but I'd acted brave. And it had worked for me, too.

Perhaps Cassie and I are alike, I thought uneasily. I didn't want to believe that, because I really didn't like Cassie at all. I hated the way she showed off all the time and twisted people around her little finger. I wasn't like that.

Was I?

I squirmed. Luckily, at that point the car radio crackled and we heard the voice of one of the police from Raven Hill, warning us that the press were waiting outside the police station.

Instantly, Cassie freaked.

She spent the rest of the drive studying her face in my mirror from all angles, to check that she was the ideal picture of a homeless kid, and fiddling with her wig. (It was pretty uncomfortable for Nick and me, but at least it stopped me from thinking all those serious thoughts.)

At the last minute I managed to get my mirror back so I

114

could brush my own hair and use some make-up on my eyes. Not that it mattered, really. Cassie nipped out of the car while Nick and I were trying to disentangle ourselves. She was posing for the press photographers before we even managed to open the car door.

Mind you, I was probably lucky that I didn't get into any of the photos because, as the flashlights on the cameras started blazing out, I spotted my parents on the edge of the crowd.

And I burst into tears again.

○

After Cassie had posed for the photographers, she was rushed into the police station to be grilled by the senior police. And on the steps she came face to face with her mother.

'Mum!' she yelled, holding her arms out. 'Oh, Mum! I thought I'd never see you again.'

'Oh, Cassie,' Hazel sobbed, as she gathered her daughter in and hugged her tightly. 'Oh, Cassie! Thank heavens you're safe.'

Nick moved over to my side and watched them with interest. 'They're really quite fond of each other, aren't they?' he said with mild surprise, sounding exactly like a scientist who was studying some mice in a laboratory.

'Of course they are,' I snapped. 'That ought to be obvious, even to you.'

'But Cassie hates Hazel interfering in her life,' Nick

pointed out. 'And Hazel often talks about Cassie as though she was some sort of performing animal, not a real person. They drive each other crazy.'

'So what?' I said irritably, holding my own mother's hand very tightly. 'They can still love each other, can't they?'

22

Sort of happy endings

Of course, there were articles about Cassie in all the papers the next day.

But the *Pen* got the story first. All because of Nick. After he'd been hugged and kissed and checked for broken bones by his mum and dad, he escaped and rang Elmo, to tell him what had happened.

So Zim held the presses and came racing down with a photographer to interview Nick and me. Just as we were finishing, Cassie and Hazel went past on their way home and Nick called out, 'Hey, Cassie, will you say a few words to the *Pen*?

Hazel said, 'Cassie isn't giving any interviews to the press until . . .'

But Cassie interrupted her and smiled at Nick. 'Don't be silly, Hazel,' she said. 'That doesn't apply to my friends.'

She sat down with Zim for five minutes and told him all

sorts of stuff about how she'd loved working with us and how we'd saved her life and how she'd never forget the time she'd spent in Raven Hill. Then she left, with Hazel following meekly along behind her.

'Why did you ring the *Pen*, Nick?' I asked curiously. 'You don't even like Elmo much.'

He shrugged. 'That's not the point. It never hurts to do someone a favour. Then you can get them to do you a favour some day, when you need it.'

That's Nick Kontellis for you. He's always totally practical. Just like Cassandra Cass. Me personally, I'm much more sensitive than they are. After a long day of running and hiding, and being jolted around the countryside in vans and cars, I just wanted to go home to bed.

Next morning, Liz turned up on my doorstep at eight o'clock, waving a copy of the *Pen*. The gang had done the delivery without me for once, of course. When I looked at the paper I saw that I'd got my photo on a front page, after all, even if it was only the front page of our local paper.

In the end, in fact, everyone did pretty well out of the kidnapping. (Except for the kidnappers, of course.) Elmo and his dad got their big scoop for the *Pen*. Nick sold his video of Cassie and the kidnappers to a TV news show for heaps of money. The Raven Hill refuge for homeless kids got some good publicity and so did The Lot, because Cassie mentioned that horrible candy bar every time she was interviewed.

And Cassie scored her big part in the drama series, just as she'd hoped. She sent all the Teen Power gang a signed photo of herself, with messages like, 'I'll never forget you, Liz' and 'You made me laugh, Tom' and 'You saved my life, Nick' and 'Thanks, Richelle.' (I don't think she liked me any more than I liked her.)

'Isn't she wonderful?' Liz sighed and I looked at her in disgust.

'Big deal,' I said. 'We saved her life and what do we get? A trip to America? A tour around a film studio, even? No way. A stupid photograph—that's all we got.'

Markham & Markham rushed their commercial for The Lot through, so that it could appear in the following week while the publicity around Cassie's kidnapping was still hot. Naturally, Cassie looked fabulous in it. She always does. The camera loves her.

The camera loved Sunny and Tom too, apparently. Luke had put in dozens of shots of them, clowning around, when they didn't even realise they were being filmed. He'd filmed Sunny walking on her hands with a The Lot bar in her mouth. He'd filmed Tom juggling with The Lot bars, and munching away on one bar while peeling off the rainbow wrapper of a second bar at the same time.

And there were one or two shots of me, moving around in the background, keeping as far away from Tom as possible.

Mum taped the ad. When you freeze frame, you can see that I'm very photogenic. The camera would love me, if it ever got the chance.

Maybe some day a famous producer will be watching TV and playing around with the remote control and he'll accidentally press the Pause button and there I'll be, smiling at him from the screen. And then he'll say: 'Find that girl for me immediately. I want to make her a star.'

Or maybe we'll have to find another film job. I'll talk to the gang about it.

Only this time, I'll tell them, I'd like a job that doesn't involve *trouble*.

That's not too much to ask, just for once.

Is it?

Raven Hill Mysteries
Emily Rodda

629924	The Ghost of Raven Hill	£2.99	❑
629932	The Sorcerer's Apprentice	£2.99	❑
629940	The Disappearing TV Star	£2.99	❑
629959	Cry of the Cat	£2.99	❑
629967	Beware the Gingerbread House (August 95)	£2.99	❑
629975	Green for Danger (August 95)	£2.99	❑

All Hodder Children's books are available at your local bookshop or newsagent, or can be ordered direct from the publisher. Just tick the titles you want and fill in the form below. Prices and availability subject to change without notice.

Hodder Children's Books, Cash Sales Department, Bookpoint, 39 Milton Park, Abingdon, OXON, OX14 4TD, UK. If you have a credit card you may order by telephone – 0235 831700.

Please enclose a cheque or postal order made payable to Bookpoint Ltd to the value of the cover price and allow the following for postage and packing:
UK & BFPO – £1.00 for the first book, 50p for the second book, and 30p for each additional book ordered up to a maximum charge of £3.00.
OVERSEAS & EIRE – £2.00 for the first book, £1.00 for the second book, and 50p for each additional book.

Name...

Address...

....

....

If you would prefer to pay by credit card, please complete:
Please debit my Visa/Access/Diner's Card/American Express (delete as applicable) card no:

Signature...

Expiry Date...

June 2

17· 23 27 34 36

37   12

May 29

3· 7 9 12 43 44

45

(5)

2 4 16 21 29 46